PRAISE
STEPHEN K

"Stephen Kozeniewski is a relative newcomer who's making a name for himself with well-crafted books that straddle the line between horror and humor…He's good at what he does."

- Don Sakers,
Analog

"I have never read anything like this. At times breathtaking and mesmerizing…"
- Frank Michaels Errington on *Hunter of the Dead*,
Cemetery Dance

"Kozeniewski is a rich voice that booms over his peers. I am coming to think of him as the closest thing to the reincarnation or spiritual successor of Ray Bradbury."

- David J. Sharp,
The Horror Underground

Copyright 2023 Stephen Kozeniewski

Cover art copyright 2023 Sharon Wasko

All rights reserved. No part of this book may be reproduced or transmitted in any form or by any means, electronic or mechanical, including photocopying, recording, or by any other mode of information storage or sharing, without the written consent of the publisher, except where permitted by law.

Names, places, characters, and incidents are the product of the author's imagination, or are used fictitiously. Any resemblance to actual events, locales, or persons, living or dead, is purely coincidental. I hope you enjoy this book I wrote about a bed. I made it myself.

For Amy

THE THING UNDER YOUR BED

"**I**'m going to eat you and your whole family."

A bubble of snot exploded in the little girl's nose as her eyes fluttered open. Had someone just spoken to her? Had she dreamt it?

"Mom?" she whispered. There was no reply. That was unsurprising. "Dad?" she tried, but, again, no response. He probably wasn't home from work yet. "Freckle?" she ventured finally, but, of course, the dog didn't speak English, so it almost certainly hadn't been him.

She glanced around the room. Nothing seemed amiss and no one was there.

Save Captain Bundrick, of course.

Bundrick had managed to wedge himself between her pillow and the headboard. She grabbed that redoubtable stuffed rabbit, yanked him out, and tucked him back under her arm. She strained her ears, trying to catch another hint of the voice which had awakened her, but at this point it was as evasive as a strand of hair in a soapy tub.

"You have longer ears than me, Cap'n. What do you think that noise was?"

She held Captain Bundrick up in front of her face and made him bounce back and forth in time to his words.

"I don't know," he responded in the low, funny voice she liked to give him. "Maybe it was just a car."

The little girl's house was on the corner of two cross streets. A traffic light stopped all the vehicles passing by on the side of the house where Mom had planted their rose bushes. Usually she didn't hear passing cars at all, even with the window open. Occasionally they drove by fast and loud, which Dad referred to as "peeling out" and Mom had once called "needledick" under her breath.

One time a car had gone by blaring a pop song. It was one of her favorite songs, not to mention one she wasn't allowed to listen to. The car had stopped at the light for a good fifteen seconds, enough for her to jump out of bed, run to the window, and dance along. Could she have mistaken a car radio for that creepy voice?

She held Bundrick up so he could peer out the window.

"What do you see, Cap'n?"

"No cars," he assured her.

Nope. A plump stinkbug was crossing her window screen at a leisurely rate, but no cars were passing through her sleepy town at this time of night. Yawning, she decided the mystery could keep until daylight. She desperately wanted to get back to dreamland.

Her dream had been a special pleasure, the kind she hated waking from and immediately wanted to fall back asleep to continue if she was disturbed. It was largely a vain hope. She was almost never able to pick up where she had left off.

In her dream she had been down at the pond in Maberry Play Park. Not just on the edge of the water, or in a bench, but actually sitting on the water, having a chat with a flock of baby ducks. The ducks had been exceedingly pleasant, and they'd played a game of Uno with regular playing cards. The little girl's mother always insisted the game was called Crazy Eights, but she preferred to call it "Uno with regular cards." Then, in a single fluid motion, the entire flock had taken wing, and she had joined them, soaring through the air, as they headed to Canada, which was where ducks went.

Then she had woken up to that strange, honey-and-turds voice.

It was rare, but sometimes she could rejoin her dreams, already in progress, and right now she wanted nothing more. She let her eyes flutter closed again. For a brief eternity she was in between worlds, unable to tell if she was awake or asleep. Certainly she couldn't move. Neither her arms nor her legs worked. She worried that if she tried too hard, they would work, and then she'd really be awake, and the ducks would be gone permanently.

And then she was right back with the ducks. Maybe it had all been a dream: the strange voice, the waking up and not being able to move, all of it. Dreams worked that way sometimes.

"Oh, I'm so glad to be back!" the little girl shouted out in joy, the wind whipping across her face as she flew through the daylight sky.

Quackers, the queen of the duck pack, turned back to look at her.

"Why, my dear," she announced in the loud British accent every queen spoke in, "whatever do you mean? You never left!"

The little girl giggled.

"Sorry, Quackers. I must have been mistaken."

"I should say so!"

She grinned. "Sorry to ruffle your feathers."

Mom, in a rare, maternal moment of not being drunk and violent, had recently taught her that term. A metaphor, Mom had called it. But here the little girl didn't use it metaphorically.

Primping and preening, and dancing around in agitation, even as they flew through mid-air, Quackers huffed and puffed her way over to the little girl and looked right in her face. Quackers's mouth opened, but instead of the duck queen's usual accented, albeit irritated tone, she spoke in the same dreadful voice which had woken the little girl earlier.

"Killing your mom and dad will be fun. But you're going to be the main course."

Black tentacles of something which was not quite smoke, not even there, really, crawled out of Quackers's mouth. The duck's eyes turned bright shining red before she dissolved entirely, replaced by the little girl's room.

Her heart raced. Her pulse pounded. A sheen of sweat coated her forehead. She couldn't move again, but this time she desperately wanted to. Her arms and legs steadfastly refused to respond. It felt like a fat little demon was crouching on her ribcage.

Sometimes this happened to her. Usually in the mornings when Mom roughly shook her awake she didn't have any problems getting up. But when she woke up in the middle of the night to pee sometimes she had to deal with this inability to move. Dr. Robert had declared it "sleep paralysis" and told her it was fairly common and not something to worry about.

Right now it was something to worry about, though. She struggled in vain until tears began running down the sides of her face in rivulets. Finally she shook the invisible demon off her chest. She wanted to gasp, but instead forced herself to breathe heavily through her mouth and nostrils.

Her eyes immediately searched the room for the source of that ghastly voice. The watery moon was full and her nightlight was on, so it was fairly easy for her to see. The light was so robust, in fact, that she could even read the titles of her favorite books on the shelf: *Where the Wild Things Are*, *Goodnight Moon*, *The Giving Tree*, and *The Very Hungry Caterpillar*, amongst others.

The rule Dad had laid down was that she was allowed to read anything she could reach. One day she dreamt of reaching the heights of taboo at the top of the nearly six-foot shelf. She imagined her parents kept the books outlining the meaning of life, what really happened to the dinosaurs, and what parents did after their children bedded down for the night there. But for now she would have to be content with tales of talking animals, sarcastic puppets, and the like.

There was nothing there. There was nothing anywhere. And she was tired. Blinking, she let her thumb settle into its natural position in the corner of her mouth. Mom often admonished her not to do that anymore, but it made as much sense as warning the ocean not to come in waves or the sun not to rise each morning. Her thumb simply fit there.

Sleepiness drifted through her room like a haze of pollen. The summer air was cool and soporific and, to be honest, the strange voice hadn't even really startled her. In the twilit realm between her dreams and wakefulness there was no danger and no fear. At least, not on a night like this.

The entire world spun away from the little girl in slow motion. Today had been a glorious day. She had carved, sanded, and painted a toy boat in the garage with Dad. This weekend, he had promised, they would attempt to set it sail in the pond at the play park. That memory had buoyed her through dinner, her bath, brushing her teeth, all the way to right now.

Unfamiliar with the concept of an out-of-body experience, she had difficulty putting words to what she was feeling. She felt almost as if she were floating up in a corner of the room. Joy, unadulterated by any responsibilities or concerns, buoyed her spirit aloft.

"I know you can hear me up there."

She sat bolt upright, her heart flitting like a hummingbird. Not sure where else to search for succor she glanced down at Captain Bundrick. The sad little rabbit's once-white fur had long since gone dunnish from wear, rather the way an adult's hair did. He was missing a button eye which Mom had often promised to replace, but apparently she had never been able to find a proper match for the right eye, nor been able to string together two sober minutes to look.

Mismatched eyes simply would not do. Captain Bundrick's dignity demanded better.

She shook him, trying to get a word of encouragement out of her leporine friend. She didn't want to do the voice for him. She wanted Bundrick to speak for himself. Bundrick, though, remained mute as always. She shook him a few more times, just to make sure, but to no effect. She glanced around the room again.

There was nothing out of sorts. Her clothes were in the hamper. Her clock sat on her bedside, its red numbers made up of nothing but interlocking red lines. She still hadn't fully learned to tell time, even digital. It confused her a bit how it could be twelve-dot dot-one-three now, but it could also be twelve-dot dot-one-three around lunchtime.

Then she felt it.

It wasn't so much an "it" to feel as it was an absence. She was too young yet to understand that there was no such thing as "cold," that the feeling of cold was in reality only the lack of heat. But somewhere in her animal mind she understood the concept. And so, now, too, did she understand what she was feeling.

There was the real world, the good and honest world, where two plus two always equaled four and cookies could be had for dessert by good little children who had not thrown a tantrum during dinner. And then there was the absence of that. Something "cold" in the sense that it lacked substance, lacked reality. Something empty the way the night sky sometimes lacked a moon and suffered all the more for it.

And that presence, or absence, really, was located directly beneath her. Three feet below, under mattress and box spring, and the wooden slats that held up both. Under her bed.

"You can pretend to ignore me if you like," the Thing Under Her Bed said, "but I'm still going to devour you. You and everyone you love."

The girl's frozen heart splashed into her stomach. She pulled Captain Bundrick in close and pinched her eyes shut.

She would refuse to answer it. She would refuse to answer it, and then it would go away. In the morning her bed would restore itself to the normal dusty, unimpressive little wooden piece of furniture which she had crawled under a hundred times before. Yes, in the morning all would be well.

She waited for an eternity, even holding her breath as long as she could. She would give it time, and the monster would disappear. That's all she had to do: wait for it to disappear.

When she could no longer stand it anymore, she opened her eyes and glanced over at the clock. It still read twelve-dot dot-one-three. Only just now as she was watching did the three flick over to a four.

A low growl rumbled through the air. It didn't really remind her of her dog, Freckle, more like the noise Ollie made when he didn't like somebody. Ollie was the pug that belonged to their next-door neighbor, Mr. Norris. Ollie decidedly did not like Mom. But the nice thing about Ollie was, all anybody had to do was stamp their foot loudly in his direction and he would run off like a scaredy-cat.

She tried to stamp her foot, but against the mattress it made no sound. She slowly slid down the bed so she could repeat the process by kicking the footboard. The growling continued, unabated. Whatever was under her bed was not going to be scared off like a pug.

The growling finally ended with a snap, like the gnashing of teeth.

An involuntary gasp escaped from the little girl's throat as she sucked in a ragged, throaty gulp of air. She instantly clapped both of her hands over her big fat mouth, but it was already too late. The monster chuckled, a low, deep rumbling almost impossible to recognize as mirth.

"I knew you were awake. I'll tell you what: I'll make you a deal. If you come down here by choice, I'll kill you before I eat you. Then you don't have to feel anything. How does that sound?"

She clenched Captain Bundrick tightly under her armpit. She had taken the poor rabbit's head off twice

THE THING UNDER YOUR BED

before by squeezing him in just that manner, but right now she didn't care. The first time, which had been years ago, Mom had grumbled, but taken him into the sewing nook for doll surgery. The second time he had just come back hastily stapled together. If she popped his head off again she didn't know what Mom would do in the morning. That is, assuming either of them were still alive.

The blanket began to shift, slowly, inexorably being tugged downwards. Obviously the Thing Under Her Bed had caught hold of a corner and was pulling. The goal was to scare her, not to actually catch her. Nevertheless, she scrambled out from under the covers and planted her bottom on her pillow.

The Thing chuckled. It was a loathsome, unwholesome noise.

"Look, the best thing for you is to just give in. What's your plan anyway? What have you got up there? A pillow? That desiccated old bunny?"

She didn't know what "desiccated" meant, but she could guess. And the Thing was right. Sort of. If it came down to a fight, she didn't really have anything to defend herself with. She glanced over at her hand-me-down desk, hopeful that something there might be useful. The desk was painted white and consisted of two levels: a writing space, and then a layer for books, but not fun books she was actually interested in, like those which lined her bookshelf. No, these were Mom's old college textbooks, some still marked with small white "Used" stickers. Mom had never finished college due to (as she often reminded the little girl) a child derailing her life.

Would one of those fat books be solid enough to battle the monster with? She wasn't sure. A box of crayons lay open on the writing surface. Those couldn't be much use, either. She could easily chew through them with her own human teeth, and the Thing Under Her Bed sounded like it had long, nasty daggers in its mouth.

Then her eyes lighted on a possibility. Mostly she colored with crayons and, when Mom let her have them, the occasional marker. But recently she had started drawing her own creations with a set of pencils in a small rectangular metal box with curved corners.

The pencils ran the gamut from very thin to very thick and each had a number on its lower end. The 8B on the far right was the thickest, she was pretty sure. She didn't entirely understand how the numbering system worked. But she was absolutely certain about one thing: she had sharpened each pencil to within an inch of its life.

She had recently received the pencil set as a gift from her grandmother. Dad (who she had gathered was actually Nana's son) had gone out to K-Mart to purchase her a pencil sharpener, which, in a lot of ways, was even more fun than the pencils themselves. She would spend minutes, sometimes, grinding away, turning the pencils from blunt cylinders to objects sharp enough to draw blood when pressed against the fleshy tops of her fingers.

THE THING UNDER YOUR BED

"Yes," the little girl said, slowly shifting her butt cheeks into a better position, "nothing but my dezizezeh rabbit and my pillow. You should come up here and see."

"That's a nice voice you've got," the Thing replied. "Very pretty. I think your vocal cords will be…mmm, just scrumptious."

She waggled her fingers through the air. They reminded her of the stingers of a jellyfish she had seen at the aquarium once. Sometimes Mom would snatch Freckle by the collar in order to take him outside. What Mom did was she just went and knelt down next to the dog, acted like she was petting him like normal, then, like a bullet out of a gun, her hand would whip out and throw the leash around the puppy's neck. Right now, that's what the little girl had to do. She had to snatch a handful of pencils from her desk before the Thing Under Her Bed could even react.

If it took the bait of her taunting, The Thing Under Her Bed would reach up, and she would just drive one of the super-sharp pencils into its hand. That would send it, howling, back into the underworld from whence it had come.

That is…if it had a hand. It could have anything. It could have stingers like a jellyfish. It could just be all teeth and nastiness. It could not even be physical, just like a fog or a mist. But then, if it were a fog or a mist, would it even be able to hurt her? She wasn't sure.

She wanted to say something through Captain Bundrick to steel her nerves, something to make her know she could do this. But she didn't want the Thing to suspect what was coming. She poised her hand and bit her lower lip, ready to snatch.

Then she stopped.

Cocked her head.

"Don't."

That had been a very different voice from the glistening nastiness of the Thing. She glanced down at Captain Bundrick. It wasn't the voice she made him talk with, either. Maybe it had just been her imagination, here in the twilight land between dreams and true wakefulness.

"What do you care if I have anything to fight you with?"

Silence.

So, she had finally shut The Thing up. She grinned over her little victory.

"Well, you're just a big bully. If you're so tough, why don't you come up here, then?"

"I'm afraid it doesn't quite work like that, little pet. No, you have to come down here. And you will. Soon enough. Along with your father and your mother and your puppy and everybody else."

She narrowed her eyes and looked to the box of pencils once again. So that was the Thing's little game.

"You're trying to distract me. Make me forget about fighting you."

"Oh, by all means, try to fight me. You should reach out and grab that pretty little second place soccer trophy from your desk there. It looks pretty heavy. You could probably bash my head in with it."

THE THING UNDER YOUR BED

"Are you *trying* to get me to reach for something?"

"I don't care what you do," the Thing sleazed, "but it would be more sporting if you could defend yourself."

Her heart rabbited. Something was off. Something was nagging at the back of her brain. Slowly, trying to make as little noise as possible, she grabbed her pillow and slowly eased the case off.

"What are you doing up there?" the Thing asked. "Grab that trophy!"

She rolled the pillowcase up into a little roll and then whipped it out, the way Dad had spanked her in the butt at the public pool once.

Something invisible, yet somehow black like ink, snapped out, whip-fast, snatching the pillowcase out of her hands. It nearly yanked her arms out of her sockets with it. Heck, it nearly yanked her off the bed with it. She crab walked with a haste she had never known possible up to the headboard.

"Aww," the Thing grumped, "this isn't delicious. It tastes a little bit like you, though. I'm getting a hint of sweat and…ooh, is that an eyelash? Delicious. I can't wait to get ahold of the rest."

She pawed at her chest. She'd never been so terrified in all her life. She could barely even see straight, and her throat was like sandpaper.

"M…M…" She clutched at her throat, unable to get any more out. It felt like there was a ball of socks lodged in there.

"Mmm, mmm," the Thing Under Her Bed repeated, mocking her, but also smacking its lips in phony hunger.

She stopped and closed her eyes. She tried to swallow, found she couldn't.

"Here," the Thing said, "let me help you. Just a guess, but were you about to say Mom?"

She didn't respond but nodded. She wasn't sure why she nodded. Nobody could see her except Captain Bundrick, and he wasn't real. The Thing certainly couldn't see her…she hoped. She had no idea why she'd nodded.

She concentrated instead on trying to swallow. It had never occurred to her how normal it was to swallow. How she swallowed all the time, a hundred times a day. And now that she couldn't, it was like not being able to breathe, or not being able to see, or she didn't know what.

"Mom?" the Thing Under Her Bed repeated, raising its voice. "Mom! Mom!"

Struggling, she pounded Captain Bundrick against the bed in frustration. Finally, she swallowed.

"Mom?" she whispered pitiably, but by this time the Thing was shouting. She raised her voice. "Mom!"

They continued in a staccato rhythm. Each time the little girl found her voice recovering a bit, the Thing shouted just that much louder, until finally they were both shouting at maximum volume until she was convinced the whole neighborhood could hear.

But not Mom. She would be passed out downstairs on the couch. Drunk, as usual, and completely dead to the world. Once, seeking a midnight snack she had walked right up and rapped mom on the forehead, just to see if it would wake her. She hadn't even stirred.

THE THING UNDER YOUR BED

The Thing continued shouting for thirty solid seconds after the little girl had already fallen silent. She hadn't given up so much as simply let herself trail off.

"What's the matter?" the Thing asked, its voice dripping with mock concern. "She doesn't seem to be coming. Do you think we should try again? Here, I'll get us started. Mom!"

"Stop," she said.

Her voice was back to normal. She was grateful for that, at least. Her pulse had stopped racing. All her fear had fled, in fact. She had burned it all off during their shouting match. Her situation was no less precarious, but at least she was back to thinking normally.

"Do you think she's blind stinking drunk, passed out on your couch? Do you think that's the issue?"

A low-pitched whine suddenly filled her ears. Excitement ran through the little girl, and hope blossomed in her heart.

"Freckle!" she cried out joyously.

The boxer was standing, proud, handsome, and erect, just outside the doorway. He wore that bleary look he got sometimes after being roused out of sleep. Even if it hadn't woken up Mom, clearly all their shouting had alerted the guard dog. She patted the mattress under her lap.

"Oh, you're in for it now. Come here, boy!"

Freckle bared his teeth and glanced under the bed.

"Yes, that's right," the little girl said, "there's something under there. Come protect me from it, boy."

She rubbed a circular area on the mattress, trying to entice the dog. Freckle nodded in acknowledgement and slowly padded into the room. His movements were short and tentative, and his head was on a swivel. He was in danger mode. Nevertheless, Freckle wiggled his butt, preparing to jump into bed with her. Technically he wasn't allowed on the bed, but Freckle usually came in after Dad fell asleep and left before he woke up, so they got away with it plenty.

"Come on," the little girl prompted. Triumphantly, she addressed the Thing Under Her Bed. "You're in trouble now. My puppers is going to rip you limb from…"

Freckle leapt. What happened next couldn't have taken longer than a second, but it seemed to transpire in decadent slow motion. Almost as soon as Freckle's back feet left the ground, his fur disappeared. For a split second he looked as silly as he had the time he had been shaved for his neutering. If his fur evaporating had been all that happened, the little girl would have giggled.

But it wasn't all.

Next, Freckle's skin sloughed off, from the tip of his tail to the namesake birthmark on his snout. His bare muscles were showing, like the model of human anatomy in the fifth grader's class at school. But then the muscles disappeared, too, hoovered away by the invisible tendrils of the Thing Under Her Bed.

All that happened as Freckle was in mid-air. Then he landed on the little girl's bed. What was left of him, anyway. The dog's bare skeleton glistened, and his intestines and inner organs peeked through his ribcage, still pulsating with life.

The dog looked up at her, his eyes still soulful and sad, reflecting the enormous pain of what had just happened to him. Somehow, someway, he was still alive, for a few moments longer, anyway.

Freckle moaned softly, a plaintive, unbearable whine.

The little girl was rooted to the spot. She didn't even know what the right thing to do was. Reach out and comfort her horribly maimed dog? Would he even understand it, without skin or fur to feel her touch? All she wanted to do, really, was get away from Freckle.

The Thing burped.

"Well, that was a nice little *amuse-bouche*," the Thing said. She didn't know what that meant. "You really must have cared about that dog." She began weeping. "Oh, yes," the Thing said, "lean over and let me taste some of those tears."

"Go to..." she started to say, "go...go leave me alone."

She found herself fumbling for words, incapable of the kind of profanity she wanted to use to hurt the Thing. She didn't even know the words she wanted to hurl at it. But, worst of all, she couldn't look away from the mangled not-quite-corpse of Freckle. She desperately wanted to, but she couldn't wrench her eyes from the wrecked thing bleeding all over her blanket.

The Thing chuckled. "Why don't you go comfort your dog? I left him up there for you. I swear to you I won't touch him."

For the first time she realized that Freckle's back paws and tail were hanging off the bed. The Thing could have easily reached up and sucked the dog under the bed as it had with the pillowcase. It was choosing not to. It had killed her dog and left it up there to make her suffer.

Freckle glared up at her accusingly as if saying, "Can't you see the pain I'm in?"

"You could kill him," a voice said.

"What?" she whispered. "What did you say?"

"I said I promise not to touch him," the Thing said.

"No, after that."

"Nothing?" the Thing ventured.

Staring down at Freckle's pained, bleeding, faceless skull, she realized she was digging her fingers into the mattress. If she took her hands away, they would have come out with two huge chunks of whatever made a mattress puffy.

"Can…can you end his suffering?" she asked, a quiver in her voice.

"Oh?" the Thing Under Her Bed asked, feigning surprise. "Is that what you want me to do?"

"Yes," she barely whispered.

"What? I didn't quite catch that?"

"Yes," she said, forcing her voice louder the way she did when Mom scolded her for not speaking up.

"Yes, what?" the Thing prompted, taking malicious joy in her discomfort, even as Freckle lay in agony.

"Yes, please," she forced herself to say flatly.

"Why, sure, of course I could."

THE THING UNDER YOUR BED

She wanted to hug her puppers, tell him it was all okay, that everything was going to be okay, but she felt nauseated just looking at him. What she really wanted was for Freckle to go away so she could stop looking at him. It was a selfish wish, and it made her feel like a terrible person, but it didn't make the longing fade in the slightest.

"Do it," she said, wiping a tear from her eye.

"Oh, sure, sure," the Thing said, its grotesque, honey-dripping voice vomiting in her ears. "Just one thing. If I do this favor for you, what'll you give me in return?"

As desperately as she wanted to, she found herself unable to close her eyes. She reached out with her foot and attempted to dislodge Freckle's body from her mattress. As soon as her sock touched the boxer's skull, she could feel how sticky it was with some kind of clear fluid mingling with blood. She hoped if she could knock the body over onto the ground, the Thing would feel obliged to go for it.

But struggle though she might, she just couldn't dislodge Freckle from his position. All he did was wail in pain as she kicked and kicked at him, increasingly less gently with each attempt. He was practically stuck to the bed with all of his juices acting as glue.

"All right, all right, hush now," the Thing said, affecting a soothing tone, though its intent was clearly not to soothe. "I'll help out first and we'll just discuss that little favor you owe me later."

Freckle yelped as one of the Thing's appendages wrapped around his rear left leg. The little girl could see it bending away like a palm tree in a hurricane wind. The Thing had been so quick and violent with the pillowcase before. Now it just seemed to be interested in prolonging her dog's suffering.

"Stop, stop!" she shouted. "Just finish it, I mean. Just...make him stop hurting."

"So demanding," the Thing said. "Very well, then."

With a hard yank, the back half of Freckle slipped over the side of the bed. The dog, in an absolute paroxysm of agony, scrabbled at the bed to try to stay put. He didn't want to go down. His lungs and intestines and other guts were sliding out of his ribcage. The little girl held out her hand, wanting to pet Freckle and yet desperately not wanting to, either.

Freckle gave her one final look of absolute betrayal before disappearing under the bed with a long, mournful howl.

She pulled her legs into her chest and wrapped her arms around them, hugging herself. She started hyperventilating. This was a nightmare. It had to be.

The worst pinches she had ever felt in her life were what her Dad called "Smurf bites." He put his thumb against the knuckle of his index finger and just pressed. She reached down, pulled up her pajama leg, and gave herself a Smurf bite.

She hissed in pain but didn't wake up. She did it again and again, and again and again, on both legs, until she was covered with tiny crescent moon-shaped bruises, all self-inflicted. She tucked her head between her legs and focused on her breath until it stopped feeling like she was drowning by inches.

When she brought her head up, she wasn't exactly calm, but she was ready to think again. Review what she knew.

The bed was like a ship. She didn't dare step off the "deck" that her mattress and blanket made. She glanced again at the pencil set on the desk. Even stretching out to grab the pencils would result in the Thing getting her, the way it had gotten the pillowcase and Freckle.

But there was something she didn't know. How fast was it? Could she distract it and run?

"That was nice what you did for Freckle," she said. "But you'd probably better take off now. Mom will wake up soon and she always finds her way to bed."

No, she didn't.

"No, she doesn't."

The little girl took the now naked pillow and ran her finger along the seam. She felt like she flipped it five times before finally locating the zipper.

"Well, it doesn't really matter," the little girl said. "The neighbors will hear. Mr. Norris probably already heard Freckle howling like that and he can't stand when he thinks a dog is in trouble. And he won't hesitate to pound on the door in the middle of the night, believe me. He and Ollie will be over shortly."

She was just talking now, rambling really, trying to keep it distracted. She didn't even know if it mattered. She didn't know if it could see her, if it even had eyes to see anything. It seemed to know about Mom and other, more disturbing things. But maybe, in a perfect world, she could outwit it, at least a little bit.

"Oh, Mr. Norris and his little dog Ollie will be over?" the Thing murmured, now adopting a faux-soothing tone. No matter how it spoke, nothing could distract from the underlying cruelty evident in its voice.

She put her fingers on the key to the zipper and began to tug. One tooth at a time came undone. She was pulling so slowly the zipper was barely making any noise. At least she didn't have to open it all the way. The Thing was chuckling now. In fact, it might have been talking and she hadn't been paying attention, so focused was she on the zipper.

"…I'm an idiot? A clown, a buffoon, down here for your entertainment? The Norrises are on the other side. Your window may be open, but it faces the street."

"Mm hmm," she replied, having run out of distraction ideas, and really just concentrating on the zipper.

"What are you doing up there?" the Thing asked, seeming to suspect something now.

Her heart leapt inside her chest. She had finally gotten the pillow unzipped enough to wriggle her little hand inside. She yanked out a handful of tiny, white feathers, each quill digging into her palm. She tossed them in a wide spray off the side of the bed.

In terror she watched as the Thing ate one feather after another. The Thing's appendages were impossible to see, but the feathers were real, and they disappeared faster than her eyes could follow. The Thing belched wetly, and a cloud of feather dust filled the air before the particles tinkled to the ground.

The little girl's heart sank.

"Oh, I get it," the Thing said, "you're testing boundaries. Like children do. Maybe I ought to come up there and spank you."

Something glinted out of the corner of her eye. A smile crossed her face.

"Then why don't you?" she asked.

There it was. A single, lone feather from the pillow stuffing had landed on the floor. It was just outside the open door of her bedroom.

"I'd much rather you come down here to join me. Or even just reach over for that…"

"Enough," she said firmly. "Stop trying to trick me. I get it now. Nothing over the edge of the bed. If I stick my hand out, you'll bite it off."

"Or snatch you down," the Thing grumbled sorely.

"And I'm guessing that extends just to the edge of the room."

"What?" the Thing snapped, unable to hide the genuine surprise in its voice. "What makes you say that? I can reach anywhere in this house. Don't think I have limitations."

"But you do," she cooed in response, "or you'd have attacked my Mom. You can't come out from under there. All you've got is the floor of my room."

It angrily yanked her entire comforter down under. She was now left with just a blanket and sheets. She grabbed them both and tugged and struggled until all the corners were no longer dangling over the side.

"I have powers beyond your ken, you little shit. Don't test me."

She wasn't sure who Ken was, but knew now wasn't the time to act uncertain.

"If you have all those great big powers," she said, "why don't you grab that feather?"

"What? Which feather?"

From her current position she was pointing, though she still wasn't sure if it could see what she was doing on top of the bed.

"Point it out to me."

She wasn't going to be fooled into sticking her hand over the side. Who knew if this creature even had eyes, or senses, or anything, really. She realized with a low thrill of terror that she had no idea what it looked like or if it had any appearance at all.

"Look towards the door," she said.

Nothing but silence emanated from beneath the bed for a spell. She stroked Captain Bundrick's graying fur, trying to keep herself calm. The silence continued for so long she leaned back against the headboard and hoped the Thing Under Her Bed had gone away, back to whatever nether realm it had come from.

"Nope," it belched up from below, "I don't see anything. Maybe you could direct me a bit better?"

"There's a feather out there," she said slowly, biting off each word. "You'll just have to trust me."

"Trust seems to be in short supply here," the Thing replied. "Maybe you could trust me and then I could trust you. Every treaty throughout history has started with one simple act of faith."

THE THING UNDER YOUR BED

The little girl paused. She liked to trust people, to reach out to them, but she had a limited capacity to do it. Always at the forefront of the little girl's mind was the time she had played hopscotch at the playground with Suzie Jennings. The other girl had stolen her chalk, simply taken it home and never admitted what she had done. People were like that. Monsters probably doubly so.

"I guess there haven't been a lot of treaties signed, then," she said.

The Thing chuckled, a mirthless, bone-chilling sound.

"Let's buck that trend, then," it replied.

"I'm much less likely to trust something that hates me."

"Hate you?" the Thing asked, attempting to sound aggrieved. "Whatever gave you the impression I hate you?"

"You promised you would eat me and my parents."

"What if that's not a bad thing? Don't you believe in Heaven?"

She furrowed her brow. Her grandmother took her to church a couple times a month. She had an idea about what Heaven was, but it had always seemed strange and hard for her to understand. Nothing was forever and nobody was ever happy for very long, so she didn't understand how there could be a place where everyone was happy forever.

"I guess," she admitted grumpily.

"Well, I'd be hastening you along to your eternal reward, my dear. What could be a more loving act than that?"

She pursed her lips. She was tired of this give-and-take, tit-for-tat. She didn't like it and she wasn't good at it. She wanted someone to just swoop in and help her. In the past, her parents had always done so. Then she remembered, it wouldn't be so long after all until one of them could.

"My Dad will be home soon," she spouted defiantly.

"Why not call out to your Mom again?" the Thing whispered in the darkness. "I'll bet she'd be delicious. I mean…a big help to you."

The little girl rubbed her forearms. Without the comforter she was getting cold. She took her blanket and carefully folded it into about a quarter of its normal size. She knew it would just barely cover every inch of her body like that, but she feared being sucked down into the writhing darkness beneath the bed if The Thing caught hold of a corner.

"Why don't you just be quiet?"

A wave of laughter from beneath the bed splashed the girl's face like cold water.

"Oh, Mum!" The Thing called out, "Mummykins! Mother dearest!"

With each word The Thing's slimy, spectral voice grew louder and louder.

"Quiet! Quiet!" the girl cried, her heart now beating solidly in her throat.

THE THING UNDER YOUR BED

"It doesn't matter! She can't hear! She's soused. It's just you and me, my darling. Now come down here and cuddle."

At that moment, the telltale noise of the door of the front door opening filled the air and a wave of relief washed over her. Dad was singing the jaunty tune he sometimes did after he'd stopped by at the local bar for a beer after work. He didn't always sing, but when he did she knew he was in a good mood.

She was so excited she rubbed her hands together feverishly like it was freezing outside.

"Dad! Dad!"

His voice drifted in from the foyer. "Hello, little people who should definitely not be awake at this ungodly hour of the night."

The thrill that shot through her spine was electric. Dad, all six feet and two hundred and fifty pounds of him, was home. He wrangled molten metal at the foundry all day. His hands were rough with calluses and harder than pumice. He wouldn't be scared of any janky old monster.

The little girl dared a peek over the side of the bed, making sure not a single fingertip or eyelash crossed the invisible barrier. She ended up having to push herself up almost onto all fours. She couldn't spot any of the ethereal nothingness she had come to think of as the Thing's substance. It had, apparently, retreated to its refuge in the blackness under her mattress.

"Not so eager to yell now, are you?"

The Thing held its peace. That was a positive change, at least.

"Dad!" she cried out again. "Dad!"

"Just a minute, cuddlebug," he responded, "I'm not ignoring you. I'll come tuck you in in a minute. I just have to take care of something first."

That meant Mom. Depending on the night of the week it was, he could sometimes get Mom on her feet and walk her like a zombie into the master bedroom. On a Tuesday or Wednesday that was still a possibility. On a Friday or Saturday, he would just cover her with a blanket and tuck a pillow that wasn't corduroy under her head.

On a Thursday like today, it could go either way. They weren't just in the phantom gray period of the night. They were in the phantom gray period of the week, too. Perhaps that was how the monster had been able to break through from its own dimension. Perhaps all of the intricacies of space and time had happened to converge on her sad little suburban home just on that night, at that particular time, in that particular place.

"No."

She looked down. She could have sworn Captain Bundrick had just spoken. It wasn't the voice she used for him. It was something else entirely, almost an independent voice.

"Did you say no?" the little girl asked.

She half expected the Thing to respond. She glanced over the side of the bed again, as far as she would dare. The writhing tentacles of nothingness that seemed to slither out from under the bed, forever on the periphery of her vision, had disappeared. And from the monster, not a peep.

THE THING UNDER YOUR BED

She shook Bundrick.

"You're scaring me, Captain," she said. "Say something. Or don't do it again."

"Who are you talking to, cuddlebug?"

Dad stood in the doorway, a silhouette in the moonlight. He flipped the switch in the hallway and pure, golden artificial light formed a halo behind him, making her blink in surprise. Finally illuminated, she could see Dad's kind face, smiling eyes, and cracked lips.

"Uh...Captain Bundrick?" she answered sheepishly.

"Oh," Dad said, nodding as though he had known all along, "and what does the captain of the good ship *Lollihop* have to say?"

All at once she felt foolish. She tucked the stuffed rabbit behind her. "Nothing."

"All right," he said. "Do you want a glass of water?"

Without waiting for a response, Dad stepped into the bathroom, which was just across the hall. She heard the spigot turn on. A moment later he returned with her glass, the one with the red dinosaurs on it. He was just about to cross the threshold into her room when she spotted the lone survivor of the feather massacre, and with it, remembered the grave danger the Thing Under Her Bed posed to everyone, Dad included. The memory of Freckle's face, torn down to nothing but bone and eyes, floated before her eyes.

"No, wait!" she shouted, waving her arm wildly through the air.

Dad stopped in mid-stride and puckered his lips quizzically.

"What's the matter, cuddlebug?"

She stared at him, her lips fluttering without making words. Staring at Dad, the man she'd seen every day of her life up until now (with the exception of two business conferences which had pulled him away for a pair of excruciating three-day periods) she realized how strange everything she had witnessed tonight seemed.

So, she'd been hearing voices. And tossed some feathers off the bed. It could all be explained away as a dream intruding on consciousness. She'd heard about such things before. Mom called them "hallucinations" and often accused her of having them, though, if she had to be honest, it seemed a lot more likely that Mom was the one suffering from hallucinations now and then.

So, her comforter was missing. She could have easily kicked it off the bed. And, with that missing, she noted, the bloody stain which was the only evidence of Freckle's disappearance was gone. Her puppers was probably even now sleeping down in the laundry room on a big pile of soiled sheets.

Maybe she had made it all up in her head. In the morning, the sunlight would come streaming in, and she would stretch her arms back behind her, and all the fear and angst of the night would seem ridiculous.

She realized, as all this ran through her head, that Dad had already passed over the threshold. Now he was standing in the weird, off-kilter, rectangular shape which the hallway light was casting upon the rug.

THE THING UNDER YOUR BED

"You don't want your water?" he asked, shaking the glass a little bit in the air.

She swallowed, hard, remembering that brief period earlier when it had been nearly impossible for her to swallow. The normalcy of that made her feel like maybe everything was getting back to normal after all.

Dad was staring at her, the kindness and worry in his face so obvious, his long shift at the foundry completely forgotten already in favor of her silly little worries. She decided she'd better level with him.

"There's a...there's something under the bed." His right eyebrow shot up, nearly rocketing through the ceiling. "Or, at least, I mean, I thought there was," she added sheepishly.

"What kind of a something?" he asked with a sort of excitement that was obviously feigned, but coming from a beloved parent, happily accepted. "A shoe? A ball, maybe?"

"No, Dad!" she cried out, surprising herself by punctuating the sentence with a giggle. "A...a...don't make me say it."

He shrugged, pantomiming an entire one-act play of confusion that made her just laugh and giggle and rock back and forth in her spot. She even pulled Captain Bundrick out from where she had stuck him to enjoy the show.

"If you don't say it, how could I possibly know what you're referring to? Is it a six-barrel Holley carburetor? The starting line of the 1976 Flyers? A screen door factory?"

As he continued proposing more and more outlandish and elaborate explanations for the mystery hidden under her bed, she finally realized how foolish she had been acting. Not just now, but all night. There was no monster under the bed. Captain Bundrick hadn't talked to her, and neither had the imaginary monster. Freckle was no more dead than she was. She had simply been dreaming, or hallucinating, or just being a very silly little girl.

Regardless of the explanation, she knew that she had to verbalize it in order to exorcise the demon. Or, better yet, have Dad exorcise the demon for her. That was what dads were for, after all, weren't they? Dads were for banishing monsters.

"No, silly billy. It's a…" she lowered her voice considerably, "…monster."

Dad looked shocked suddenly and made a distinctive screeching sound with his mouth. He'd called the noise a "record skip" once but had never explained to her what a record was or what it might be skipping.

"A monster?" he repeated, filling his voice with feigned awe.

The little girl nodded wildly, Dad's presence filling her with confidence that it had all been in her head. She glanced down at Captain Bundrick briefly. Rather than staring up at her with reproach, he was just a dumb old stuffed bunny, every stain from every bit of food or grease she had spilled on him over the years clearly visible even in the subdued light.

THE THING UNDER YOUR BED

Dad ran his hand under his chin, feigning a deep thought process.

"Well, now, this is a dilly of a pickle. Monsters are not easy to kill. Not easy to kill at all. What kind did you say it was?"

"What kind what?"

"Well, what kind of monster, silly? Is it a vampire? Because then I'll have to go and pull a tomato stake out of the garden."

The little girl shook her head. "No, I don't think so."

"Is it a werewolf? I think your mom might have some silver jewelry in the drawer." The little girl giggled. "Is it a bigfoot?"

"Dad!" she protested loudly.

"Well, if it's a bigfoot, all I have to do is go get my shotgun. I'll take care of him lickety-split. Would you like that?"

She bit her lower lip, then nodded. Usually when they played these sorts of chicken games, she was the one to blink first. Dad was staring at her, an unusual look on his face. He hadn't been expecting that.

"You…really want me to do that?" he repeated, inquiringly.

She nodded again, much more emphatically this time. She was convinced the Thing Under Her Bed was false: nothing more than what her parents sometimes called a "delusion" when they thought she couldn't hear them. Sometimes she sat at the top of the stairwell, her legs poking between the balusters defiantly, as they fought about the things she talked about with Dr. Robert.

They used the word "delusion" often, and sometimes, "hallucination." She always scampered away before Dad came up the stairs, and so far, had never been caught. But she knew what they really thought of her. Knew that Mom thought she was a "deranged little fuck" and that Dad sometimes questioned whether he was even really her father. She'd heard it all and they had no idea.

Dad nodded and walked away. Suddenly, panic fluttered in her heart again.

"Wait, Dad!" she cried out.

"I'll be right back, cuddlebug," his voice sounded from just down the hall.

"Oh," she replied, "okay."

In the stillness, her voice seemed to echo a thousand times louder than ever before. She heard Dad stomping out to the garage. He had never been one not to play along with her. She had wanted to ask him to bring Freckle back with him. Seeing her dog safe and sound would've made all her fears just melt away.

"What is your plan with all this nonsense?"

The Thing was back.

"You're not real," she said flatly.

"Ohhhh," the Thing said, stretching the ululating syllable out into a symphony of length, "is that what you're trying to convince yourself of?"

She paused, flipping Captain Bundrick's head back and forth.

THE THING UNDER YOUR BED

"There's no 'convincing' involved," she said. "I'm crazy. That's what Dr. Robert says. That's what my parents say, too, when they think I'm not listening."

Captain Bundrick turned his head and looked up at her. He spoke like a military man, in short, clipped sentences.

"You're not crazy," the rabbit stated flatly.

She held him up to her face. His lips weren't moving.

"That's rough," the Thing said. "Listen kid, I'm sort of honor-bound to devour you and destroy all of your loved ones. But that doesn't mean I necessarily enjoy it. I don't like hurting people who are already hurting. Let's just get this over with, shall we? It'll just be, you know, a spot of messy business we both have to push through. But we'll get through it together, what do you say?"

"So you don't think I'm crazy?" she asked, ignoring the Thing and directing her question to Bundrick.

"Huh?" the Thing said.

"Shhh," she hissed, "I'm not talking to you."

"Certainly not," Bundrick responded crisply. "I've served as your companion for how long now?"

"Years," she replied.

"Who...who are you talking to up there?" the Thing asked, its voice trembling, if that was even possible.

"And in all that time," Bundrick continued, "I have never seen anything to make me believe that you didn't have your wits entirely about you."

"You really mean it?" she asked.

Salty tears of relief formed in the corners of her eyes.

"What?" the Thing asked, sounding confused, as much as it could in that dark, succulent voice, "There's nobody up there. Your Mom's drunk, your Dad's out in the garage…"

The Thing continued talking, but she stopped listening.

"I do," Bundrick replied, his voice not seeming to rise, yet still, somehow, drowning out the Thing. "I think you're as sane as they come. I wouldn't have staked my claim in this world on you if I believed otherwise."

She squeezed the little bugger tight in her arms, almost crushing him, almost causing his poorly stapled head to pop off.

"All right, all right," he said, his voice not seeming to be muffled, despite his head being tucked way up under her armpit, "that's enough of the mushy stuff."

"Figures," the Thing muttered. "All the beds in the universe to choose from and I get stuck under one that belongs to a fucking lunatic."

She heard the front door opening again, then the screen door slamming shut. Dad was back.

"You're in for it now," she said triumphantly.

The Thing didn't respond. She was almost tempted to lean over the side to check if it was still there. Almost. It seemed that every time Dad showed up, it suddenly didn't want to talk anymore. He appeared in

THE THING UNDER YOUR BED

the doorjamb, the shotgun he had only let her see three times and touch once tucked under his arm.

She wasn't stupid. She knew the weapon wasn't loaded. But the fact that he had gone to get it to put her mind at ease made her feel much better about things.

Dad smiled deftly, his toothy grin suddenly overtaking the rest of his face.

"Right," he said, "so, time to take out this bigfoot – or bigfeet – of yours, what do you say?"

"Wait, Dad," the little girl said, holding up her arm.

He cocked his head to the side.

"What is it, cuddlebug?"

"You should load it, Dad," she said firmly. "I'm serious."

Dad nodded, the little tip of his tongue sticking out of the side of his mouth. He shook the weapon in her direction, though, tellingly, never let the barrel stray from being firmly pointed at the floor.

"Of course it's loaded," he said. "I loaded it in the garage. Wouldn't be much use to us unloaded, now would it?"

She knew he was lying but nodded in acceptance. She had warned him. Multiple times. She glanced down at Captain Bundrick.

"It'll be all right," Bundrick said.

"I know," she said, stroking the silly bunny's ears.

"What's that, cuddlebug?"

"I was saying I know it'll be all right now. Now that you're here, Dad. Captain Bundrick was worried."

"Oh, was he now?" Dad asked, finally crossing over the threshold for the first time into her room.

The little girl winced in worry. Now that he had passed the doorjamb, he was completely vulnerable to the Thing Under Her Bed. He could be snorted up, just like Freckle. But no absorbing tentacles flitted out to assault him. She relaxed. Dad even came close enough to run his hands along Captain Bundrick's head.

"Well, not to worry, Cap'n. The cavalry's here. Now let's see what we've got under here."

Dad went to his knees before her bed, as though he were praying.

"Goodness," he said, "What's happened to your comforter?"

"The Thing Under My Bed took it," she said, before clamping her hands over her mouth. She didn't know if, like a demon, mentioning its name would give it power. But, then, that was just what she called it. She had no idea if it really had a name or not.

"Oh," Dad said, and she could tell he was trying not to roll his eyes, "the comforter's under the bed, eh? Maybe I'll fish it out for you while I'm checking for monsters, then, eh?"

She nodded and he nodded in response. He was acting as though he had figured out the real reason she had asked him to check under her bed, even though there really was a monster under there. Or, at least, before Dad had arrived with his gun and the lights of the outside world, it had seemed that way.

Dad lifted the dangling blanket and stuck his head under the bed.

"Ohhh, I don't see anything," Dad's muffled voice said. "Any monsters down here? No? Oh, wait!" The

THE THING UNDER YOUR BED

little girl nearly jumped through the roof, leaving a Bugs Bunny-shaped hole. "Oh, no, not a monster," Dad reported, "a dust bunny. Lots and lots of dust bunnies. Major Rabbit must have some friends down here."

"Captain Bundrick," she corrected, and the captain himself weighed in on the matter at the same time. She giggled as their voices mingled.

"I don't see the comforter, though," Dad said. "You sure you dropped it down here?"

"No," she said, "I told you, Dad, the Thing Under My Bed took it."

"Right, right," Dad agreed absently, "The red-eyed monster took it."

"Red-eyed?" she repeated in confusion.

"Didn't you say that?"

"No," she said, "I don't even know if it has eyes."

He straightened up with a grunt, clutching at his back. "I can't see a thing under here in this dim light."

He placed the shotgun tentatively on the side of her bed and gave her a look as if to say, "You know you're not allowed to touch this." She nodded her assent.

He reached into his pocket, pulled out his cell phone and activated the flashlight app. She shielded her eyes. The light streaming in from the hallway was fine(ish). It was dim enough from such a distance not to hurt her eyes. But the flashlight was shockingly bright and made her snap her eyes shut.

"Nope, nothing," she heard Dad say.

She tried to open her eyes again, but a swarm of bruises dancing through the air made it impossible.

"Hang on a minute. What's this?"

Suddenly, a sound like a whirring blender filled the room. The light disappeared and she was able to open her eyes again. She blinked rapidly, trying to clear her vision.

The cell phone had fallen out of Dad's hands and lay now, face down on the floor by his kneeling form. His entire torso and head were under the bed. Dad's leg kicked out, once. Then it began twitching.

"Dad?" she whispered, all the moisture disappearing from her mouth.

In an instant his twitching leg turned into a kicking leg, like a grasshopper's. Then his whole body began to writhe and shake. The whirring grew louder and louder and then in the space of a split-second his entire body was sucked under the bed. Only his screams and the strange buzz of the devouring monster filled the air.

The little girl stared, open-mouthed, aghast.

"Stop squeezing me," Bundrick wheezed in her arms, before she had realized she was clenching him so tightly the staples in his neck were beginning to buckle.

"D…D…" she tried to articulate.

A plume of blood exploded out from under the bed spraying the floor, her Sunday shoes, the wall, everything.

The little girl began to scream. She screamed loudly, not caring what the neighbors would think. Not caring what her Mum would think, if it broke through her drunken torpor at all. She screamed and screamed for all she was worth at the horrible, bloody demise of her Dad.

"Enough of that."

THE THING UNDER YOUR BED

She glanced down at Bundrick, who was standing of his own volition and staring at her. His remaining button eye didn't blink, but otherwise he seemed fully alive. She'd spoken for him often enough in the past. And tonight he had even begun speaking on his own. But this was the first time she'd ever seen him move.

"Cap'n…how are you…?"

"Never mind," the stuffed rabbit said, "that's not what's important now. What is important is that The Thing Under her Bed doesn't escape."

"Who are you talking to up there?" the monster intoned. "I know it's not your father."

It cackled deliriously.

Her hand was shaking violently, but she slowly placed it on the barrel of the shotgun. Dad had let her see it a few times, even let her touch it once, but she had no idea how to use a gun, outside of what she had seen in the movies. Besides, it wasn't loaded. Was it?

"I'm…" she said, and was instantly shocked by how absolutely calm and assured her voice sounded, before continuing, "I'm speaking with my friend, Captain Bundrick."

"The fucking bunny rabbit?" The Thing Under Her Bed practically howled. "Not this again. Remember what your headshrinker told you."

"My head what?"

"Your shrink. You don't know that word? Your psychiatrist. Psychologist. Whatever. Doctor…what'd you say his name was?"

"Robert," she supplied.

"Yeah," The Thing agreed greasily.

She looked down at Captain Bundrick. He was carefully examining the weapon, marching around it like a real soldier. Or, at least, how she imagined soldiers really marched, lifting his legs high, with his tiny, fingerless hands tucked behind his back.

"He said you're fucking dotty, right? So don't listen to your stuffed rabbit. He's clearly a delusion."

She looked at Bundrick, a pleading look in her eyes. Bundrick sniffed huffily.

"An equally compelling counter-case could be made that the Thing Under Your Bed is the delusion."

Still not daring to let even the tips of her fingers dangle over the side of the mattress, she tried to glance down at the Thing.

"Yeah," she said, "what about that?"

"What about what?" the Thing replied.

"Maybe you're imaginary. Maybe Bundrick's the real one."

"Oh, really?" the Thing cooed. "Well, tell me this: what happened to your father? Whose blood is that spattering the wall? Could a hallucination do that? What happened to your beloved dog? Aren't your sheets still sticky from his guts?"

She looked at Bundrick. Bundrick reached his hand up to his face. Had he had fingers, he probably would have been pinching his nose. Instead, he simply shook his head.

"This is a circular argument. If you're mad, as you might be – certainly are, in fact, because one of us, either myself or the monster must necessarily be an illusion – then the disappearances of your father and

THE THING UNDER YOUR BED

your dog could also have been hallucinations. Macbeth famously saw blood that was not there, a knife that did float in the air."

"I remember," she said.

"Remember what?" the Thing asked. "Christ on the can, it's like talking to a mental patient under here."

"Dad explained about the knife in the air to me when we watched the old black-and-white movie," she continued, ignoring the creature's outburst.

Bundrick nodded. "What time does your father normally get home?

"Midnight," she said.

"Oh, it's after midnight now, baby girl," the monster hissed, chuckling.

She glanced at the glowing alarm clock. It was right. One dot dot zero six.

"Well," Bundrick said, "I'm willing to concede that maybe your father did come home and that monstrosity under your bed killed him. But he could also just still be at the bar. Everything that's transpiring tonight could be an illusion. You could even simply be dreaming."

"Yes," she agreed, "this is all a dream."

"I'm not a dream," the Thing muttered.

The girl scrunched into the headboard, hugging her knees again. She felt a soft, almost reassuring pat on her thigh. Bundrick.

"What are we going to do, Cap'n?" she asked.

"Enough with the rabbit bullshit," the Thing Under her Bed moaned.

Bundrick held his arm out as if to snap his fingers, although, of course, he had no fingers. A snapping sounded nonetheless.

"Hey," he said, "don't listen to it. Don't listen to it anymore tonight. Put it entirely out of your mind."

"But I can't," she hissed. "It's tormenting me, driving me crazy."

"Driving you?" the Thing said, following it up with an epic peal of laughter. "Little girl, you were as mad as a hatter before I ever met you."

"You see?" she said to Bundrick, pointing a damning finger groundward.

Bundrick put on a resolute air. "Whatever he says, you don't listen to him anymore. Only listen to me."

"All right," she said quietly, "I'll only listen to you."

"Hey, how about this?" the Thing said. "I've got places to be, people to eat. I can't spend all night hanging out here, you know. So how about I make you a proposition? If you come down here of your own accord, I'll leave your mother alone."

The little girl stared at Bundrick. The rabbit lowered his head, slowly, mournfully.

"It might be for the best," she said.

"Of course it would be for the best," the Thing cooed. "You've already lost your dog and your father thanks to your inability to handle this situation on your own. Now I'm practically offering you an olive branch on a silver platter. I'll spare the life of your last remaining loved one. You just come down here of your own accord. Trickery is all right, you know? But a

THE THING UNDER YOUR BED

willing sacrifice is so delicious. You can't even understand."

"Block him out," Bundrick stated flatly.

"I don't know," she hissed, putting her hands over her ears.

She wanted to block it out. Block everything out. Bundrick, the Thing, the blood spatter on the wall which had formerly been Dad, the sticky part of her sheets which had formerly been Freckle, all of the terrors and nightmarish monstrosities of the night. She just wanted to close her eyes and fly around with Quackers the British duck, and when she woke up it would be morning and everything would look all right in the light of the sun shining in through the window.

"Don't listen to him," Bundrick repeated, "only listen to me."

She nodded. Taking a deep breath, she attempted to block everything out. The Thing was still talking, but only snippets of what it was saying came through.

"…a hero…save your mother…the woman who gave you life…"

"All right," she agreed, "I'm only listening to you. What do you have to say?"

Bundrick nodded as if acknowledging a truth universally accepted, but one that a donkey like her had to be dragged to against her own will. In response to her question, he simply turned and stared at the gun.

"…epic," the Thing was saying, its voice occasionally piercing her self-imposed cloud, "…wouldn't it…we can all move along with our lives…"

She reached out, her fingers fluttering like they each had lives of their own. She let her middle finger settle on the cool metal of the weapon's barrel. Something like a mousetrap snapped her finger.

She flinched away as if she'd been burned. She had actually been burned once, on a hot stovetop. It had been extraordinarily unpleasant. She stared down now at her finger, which was thrumming with the memory of that long-ago pain, but it wasn't the same as what had just struck her.

"Don't be afraid to touch it," Bundrick admonished.

"I'm not afraid," she replied.

"Oh, you're not?" the Thing said, its voice suddenly coming into focus like the world did when she put on her glasses each morning. "Well, you should be, you little shit. You have no idea the universe that is out there, aching to devour you. All reality will happily gobble you up. You should have been terrified from the day you were born."

"Ignore him," Bundrick said. "You don't have to do anything except touch it. Just touch the gun."

"I'm not afraid," she reiterated, "but something just bit me."

She realized, staring at her hand, that she'd been shocked, as sometimes happened when she touched a doorknob after scampering around the house in her footie PJs at Christmastime. Dad had explained to her all about static electricity once when that had happened, how a single electron jumped from one atom that had too many in the doorknob to one atom that had too few

THE THING UNDER YOUR BED

in her hand. She had found it all fascinating, if a bit doubtful, but her teacher had even confirmed the assertion later in science class.

The little girl stared down at the shotgun laid out before her like a Thanksgiving feast. She understood, respected, and feared the power of such a device. Dad had drilled that into her head repeatedly. So maybe it wasn't so bad. Maybe she could be responsible and touch it.

She extended her arm again. This time her fingers didn't waggle. Slowly, as though petting a dog she was worried would spook and run away, she placed her palm on the wooden stock of the gun. This time she wasn't stung.

"That's good," Bundrick said. "See, it won't hurt you."

"It certainly *could* hurt me!"

"Is that your worry?" the Thing cooed, attempting to put on an air of concern, "getting hurt? I could make it so painless for you. You and your mother both. You have my word, my absolute word. It'll be like a pinprick through the back of your neck. You won't feel anything, just a light tap, and then all your senses will be dead."

She stuck out her lower jaw and bit her upper lip, teeth stretched out like Frankenstein. She looked at Bundrick and mouthed the words "I hate him."

Bundrick nodded in agreement. "I'll walk you through it. Put your hand on the wooden part at the bottom, that's the stock, and your other hand on the metal part, that's the barrel."

"Yes. I remember. Dad told me."

"Your father told you what?" the Thing rumbled.

She took the weapon in the manner Bundrick described. She went to her knees and braced herself as best she could. The weapon was almost as big as she was.

"Now do you remember what kind of action this is?"

"Break," she replied.

"You need a break, little darling?" the Thing asked with a chuckle. "A few minutes to make a decision without me whispering in your ear? Maybe that could be arranged. I'm just here to make you comfortable with your decision."

"You need to break it," Bundrick said, "and check if Dad actually loaded it."

"He didn't," she said, and waited for the Thing to comment on her one-sided conversation with Bundrick, but it remained silent. She wasn't entirely sure if it was feigning ignorance of what the stuffed rabbit was saying or genuinely couldn't hear him.

"If he hasn't," Bundrick said, "then we're no better off than we were five minutes ago. But if he has, then it could mean the difference between life and death."

She nodded. She pointed at a small metal button on the side of the shotgun.

"Just press here?" she asked.

Bundrick nodded flatly.

She put her finger on the button and pressed slowly, so infinitesimally slowly that she was barely doing anything at all. She imagined out in the woods hunting or wherever, pressing the button was meant to be quick. But she didn't dare let the Thing get wise to Bundrick's plan. Besides, she'd had plenty of practice with silencing her movements in the dark.

Years ago, Mom hadn't simply passed out after drinking every night. She would remain awake and belligerent. In those days, if she ever got caught doing something after lights out Mom would scream at her and berate her sometimes for hours.

And so, out of necessity, she'd learned how to wriggle her body, millimeter by millimeter out of the bed so that the mattress wouldn't creak. Then she'd open the door, bracing both sides with her hands, so slowly that even its rusty hinges wouldn't creak, which was really quite an accomplishment. Then on the barest of tiptoes she'd whisper across the hall, all so she could pee in absolute silence without turning on the lights, and not flushing until morning.

All of this ran through her mind as she barely depressed the button on the shotgun.

"Still alive up there?" the Thing asked. "Thinking? Praying?"

She only knew one way to pray. That was on her knees, palms pressed flat against each other, hands perfectly vertical and pointed toward the sky, head bowed, and repeating words she'd memorized by rote. She wasn't sure how any of that would work with a shotgun in her grip.

"No, not dead," she said, continuing to just barely activate the weapon's action. "Not praying, either. I'm wondering, though, what should I call you?"

"Ah," the Thing said, "not dead and not praying. Only stalling. You have no need to call me anything, my darling one. But what should I call you?"

Names had power. Wasn't that the point of *Rumpelstiltskin*? She didn't care to give hers up.

"You have no need to call me anything, either. I'm nothing to you, isn't that right? Just another helpless child on your long parade of terror?"

With a long-sought and hard-won silence, the breaking mechanism of the shotgun came apart. She worried as the barrel came tumbling down that it would make noise, but the front sight merely bounced off her blanket before coming to a rest, silent as the grave. Her eyes widened. She could see the coppery bottoms and red plastic bodies of two – two! – shells, one loaded into each barrel of the shotgun. She stared down at Bundrick who, though he had no mouth save a semicircle of thread, seemed to be smiling.

"A helpless child," the Thing Under Her Bed said, after clucking its tongue, or, perhaps imitating that noise, as she wasn't entirely convinced it had a tongue. "Come down here, then, helpless child. Show me how helpless you really are."

Setting her jaw, she braced the barrel of the shotgun and leaned into the stock, slowly pressing the two halves back together.

"Coming," she answered the Thing in a sing-song voice.

She held her breath as she knew the two pieces of the shotgun were coming back into contact. Using the bed as a brace, she continued to push, and then,

THE THING UNDER YOUR BED

astonishingly, they came back together with no more than the tiniest portion of a click.

But it was enough.

"What was that?" the Thing asked.

"I didn't hear anything," she said in a teasing voice nearly approximating the Thing's own. "What did it sound like?"

She gestured at Bundrick, the serious look on her face a complete departure from the treacly falseness of her tone. She pointed to two spots, silently asking the question, "Through the bed or over the side?"

Over the side was dangerous. The Thing might spot the weapon, might even be able to reach up and snatch it out of her hands.

Through the bed? She wasn't sure about that, either. Who knew if a shell would penetrate her mattress, box spring, and the wooden slats which held her box spring off the floor. Even if a shell could pass through all that, if her aim was off, it might still accomplish nothing.

"It sounded," the Thing susurred slowly, "like a little beaver getting too busy for her own britches."

Bundrick pointed definitively at the mattress. She cocked her head inquisitively, but with his little, fingerless hand he pointed again. "It'll go through. I promise."

She nodded.

"You should be working overtime to placate me," the Thing said, returning to its earlier train of thought. "I could make things very easy for you, you know. Or very hard. I'm capable of great mercies. And great torments. The choice is yours, really."

She pointed at a spot in the center of the bed. Bundrick shrugged. She pointed at another, just to the left of the first. Bundrick nodded, but not entirely in approval.

"If you think I'm going to start being nice to you, you're crazy.

"Oh, cuckoo for Coca Puffs, am I?" the Thing asked, affecting a strange, silly voice, one that she had never heard before. She didn't respond. "Do kids still know that commercial?"

"What's a commercial?" she asked.

Splitting the difference, she pointed the shotgun at a spot in between the first two. Bundrick shrugged, as close to an affirmation as he seemed willing to give. She pressed the front sight of the shotgun into the mattress until it had no more give. As she was about to squeeze the trigger, Bundrick held up a hand. She imagined he was holding up a single digit, as people sometimes did when trying to halt one another, though, of course, Bundrick had no digits.

"Oh, so it's like that, eh?" the Thing asked. "You're going to make me feel old just because I was around a billion years before this ocean rolled?"

She let a small space appear between the front sight of the gun and the blanket. Bundrick took the barrel, moved it what felt like a millimeter, then looked up at her and nodded. She pressed the shotgun back into the spongy mattress.

THE THING UNDER YOUR BED

"Yeah, I guess so," she said, pausing to wipe the sweat that seemed to be cascading from her brow despite it being otherwise a cool summer's night.

She pressed the recoil pad into her shoulder and clenched her teeth. She wrapped her hand around the trigger guard and was surprised to find there were two triggers.

"Which one?" she mouthed.

Bundrick shook his head. "Doesn't matter. Either. Or both."

She nodded.

"Well, my dear," the Thing was saying, "I could wax poetic for the rest of the night about all the fads your kind have been through. And by 'your kind' I mean children. Breakfast cereals and Saturday morning cartoons, and before that there was a ball in a cup and long before that, children were very interested in sweeping. I know, it sounds silly now, but there was something about sweeping out a cave that kids just thought was absolutely…"

Whatever the children of primitive man thought about sweeping a cave was blasted away by the roar of the weapon discharging.

The little girl flopped backwards on her butt, her ears ringing and her shoulder wailing in pain. She wanted to cry out but was too stunned. Bundrick was slapping at the sheet, which had caught fire. Her shoulder throbbed with pain, far worse than even Mom could deliver when punching at full strength.

She yawned, deliberately opening her mouth, but her ears felt like they were plugged with cotton. It felt like a solid minute before her hearing grudgingly came crawling back, ebbing in and out like the waves at the ocean. It seemed that there was nothing, then the vague sounds of the street outside and the cicadas flowed back in. With a start, she realized Bundrick was calling for her, and probably had been non-stop.

"What?" she hissed, shocked at how little she could hear her own voice.

"What are you doing?" the stuffed rabbit protested anxiously, his voice coming in waves along with every other noise. "You've lost the shotgun!"

She looked around. It was nowhere to be seen. She scrabbled at the blanket, searching for it. She even tossed the blanket up in the air to make sure it wasn't hidden somewhere underneath. But of course it wasn't. She glanced over the side of the bed. There it lay, the great, gleaming weapon, smoke still issuing from its barrel.

She stared at it. She stared at it so hard, she thought she might burn a hole through it. She swallowed a lump in her throat.

"He...hello?" she asked, her voice still sounding in her ear canals like a dull, distant echo.

No answer came. Had she really killed The Thing Under Her Bed? Was it possible?

Perhaps she had only scared it. She looked to Bundrick.

"Is it over?" she asked.

"I don't know," Bundrick replied.

"Nothing could have survived that," she said.

THE THING UNDER YOUR BED

She had seen Dad shoot pheasants, ducks, and, occasionally, an entire aluminum coffee can with it before. He had warned her, in no uncertain terms, how dangerous the shotgun was, that, though it was a tool, it could hurt or even kill her, and was not to be used lightly. He had even given her the speech about how it could be used to stop a bad guy – but that she had to be absolutely, 100% certain that somebody was going to attack her or her own before she used it in earnest.

Well, she had been 100% certain. Dad's brains and blood were spattered against the wall. Her blanket was still sticky with Freckle's remains. The Thing Under Her Bed had already come for her and hers. She nodded. She had done the right thing in taking it out.

"Well," Bundrick said, toeing the edge of the bed, "I suppose we ought to go call the police. Or try to wake your mother. But if that shotgun blast didn't wake her, I don't know if anything will." She nodded. Call the police. 911. Both of her parents had taught her that number. It was easy to remember. "I suppose you can't leave the shotgun there."

She nodded in agreement. She joined him at the edge of the bed on her knees, staring down.

"I should pick it up," she agreed.

"Yes," Bundrick agreed after a moment's reflection, "you should."

"Or you could," she added.

"Well, somebody'd better pick up the goddamned shotgun."

The little girl clasped her hands over her mouth. That voice. She'd hoped beyond hope and been wrong. The Thing was still down there.

"Well, I tried," it declared, its nasty voice cutting right through her lost hearing. "I tried to lay low and give you a moment to reach your hand over the side. But even when you thought I was dead you wouldn't take the bait. So, I guess it's time to take another approach."

One of its dark, invisible, unknowable appendages reached out and placed itself on the shotgun.

"No!" the little girl shrieked, and almost reached out to grab the shotgun, if only to keep it out of the Thing's clutches.

It waited, at least ten seconds too long, flexing the shotgun, acting like it was pulling it under. She had seen it snatch feathers out of the hair, and the skin right off her dog. It wasn't this slow. It was playing with her, toying with her. She exchanged a glance with Bundrick.

"What do I do?" she asked.

"Come grab your father's weapon. He couldn't protect you when he was alive, but maybe in death he could be less of an abject fucking failure."

She didn't like all the swear words the Thing used. And she had no idea what "abject" meant, although she guessed it was another swear like the f-word.

She looked to Bundrick for guidance. He shook his little head ruefully.

"You know what happens if you put your hand over the side."

"But we can't let it have the shotgun."

THE THING UNDER YOUR BED

"I think we have no choice," Bundrick said.

"Oh, yes, we can," the Thing said, right over top of Bundrick's words. The shotgun slowly slithered under the bed. "And now, it seems, my dear, the tables have turned. You like shooting at me so much? Maybe it's time you found out what it feels like."

She cringed at the sound of the shotgun unhinging.

"Well, well," the Thing said, "only one shell left. I guess maybe that's fair. You did only get one shot at me."

A loud, metallic click sounded. She wasn't a hundred percent sure, but she thought maybe it had pulled the trigger on the empty barrel. Up until a few minutes ago she hadn't realized shotguns had two triggers, but she guessed it made sense. The sound still made her flinch, even though it wasn't a rip-roaring explosion.

"Oh, you didn't like that, did you?" the Thing asked. "I could see you shifting like you didn't like that noise. You don't like it when you know someone has a gun and they have it pointed at you, do you?"

The same clicking noise sounded again. Yes, the Thing must have been pulling the trigger on the empty barrel.

"Yeah, it must be really unpleasant for you up there," the Thing said, "to have someone threatening you. The only thing worse, I would imagine, is not knowing someone's pointing a gun at you. At least this way you're expecting it."

The click came again. This time she didn't flinch.

Bundrick tugged on her pajamas, but she brushed the little stuffed animal away. Another click came. She flattened her ears trying to catch where it had come from. Where was the Thing pointing the gun?

She pointed at Bundrick and then at her own ears. "Listen," she was saying. But Bundrick was gesticulating urgently. He wanted to tell her something. She shook her head. "Listen," she signaled again.

"Oh, boy," the Thing said, "it's getting quiet up there. Here, want me to break the silence?"

This time, instead of clicking the trigger, it broke the action again. The sound was jarringly unexpected, and the little girl clenched her teeth. She glanced at Bundrick, who was now dutifully circling the bed, trying to listen and echolocate where the sounds were coming from, and therefore be able to tell where the Thing had the gun pointed. Bundrick pointed at a spot near the center of the bed.

She realized with a start that the bed was no longer a solid barrier. She had punctured a thousand little holes in it herself. No light escaped the holes, but, then, there was no source of light under the bed. Quite the opposite, in fact. If she peered into one of those holes – and she dared not – she feared all she would see would be a fuller, more perfect darkness than she had ever imagined.

She scrunched away from the spot Bundrick was indicating, and tried, too, to avoid the holes from the many shotgun pellets. Bundrick was avoiding the area, too, but at the foot of the bed. So, they were separated now.

THE THING UNDER YOUR BED

"Got nothing to say?" the Thing asked.

She nodded and swallowed a lump in her throat. She prepared to give an entire speech to the Thing. She wasn't sure why, wasn't sure, even in that moment, what she intended to say, whether she meant to reason with it, scare it, convince it, or just distract it. Perhaps a little of each. But only one word escaped her lips.

"Listen…"

This time, there was no click. Or, rather, there was, but then it was followed by an earth-rending boom.

She realized her mistake. The whole time the Thing had been in possession of the shotgun she hadn't said a word. It had been waiting, apparently, for her to speak. And now it had perfectly located her by the sound of her voice.

Well, maybe not perfectly. She was still alive, after all. But she had been stung by dozens of tiny particles of buckshot. Her leg and elbow were bleeding, badly. A pool of blood gathered on her sheet. Her eyes fluttered, and though she didn't want to, she pitched forward, her head not even landing on her pillow.

"You're a funny looking duck," the little girl said, each word coming out slowly, lazily, the way it did from Mom when she was very drunk but still upright.

Quackers bristled at her words. She stood, hunched over a campfire built in a solid stone pit. The queen of the ducks was warming her hands – wings, the little girl supposed – by the flame. The night was bright, clear, and moonless. All of her ducklings lay in piles around the two of them, snoring loudly.

"You really are an uncouth little human," Quackers said, pecking away at something under her wing, "but at least I have the general decency not to point that out."

"I'm not really here," the little girl said, noticing how strange and distant her voice sounded, "I'm dying in the real world, I think."

Quackers hopped a few times around the firepit. "Well, are you or aren't you?"

The little girl looked down at her leg. It was dripping with blood, dark and inky in the low light. "I think I am."

"Well, what are you going to do about it?"

"I think I'm going to die."

"You could," Quackers mused, "or you could fight. The choice is yours."

The little girl picked up a stone and tossed it toward the lake, which seemed to have a great, white moon submerged within it. Her stone skipped across the lake perfectly.

In truth, she had never been able to get a stone to skip before. Dad had tried to teach her how to do it, but every time she had attempted, the stone had just sunk like, well, a stone. But here, in her dreamscape, which she increasingly recognized as false, her stone not only skipped across the lake but continued skipping across the beach on the far shore, then off into the distance.

She leaned back, placing her head on the edge of the firepit, using the stone like a pillow. Blood kept dripping from her pantleg. She watched as the stone she had set to skipping earlier skipped by her again, presumably after its first full circuit of the earth. Quackers strutted around, ducking her head beneath her wing and pecking away at something down there.

"What are you doing?" the mother duck asked.

"Laying here," the little girl muttered.

Quackers strutted up onto her chest. She was reminded, all of a sudden, of the force which had held her down in her bed earlier. In the real world sleep paralysis had probably set in for her, but she didn't want to think about that.

"How long are you going to lay there?"

"Until I'm dead," the little girl said, crossing her arms so the duck couldn't walk any further up her chest.

"Mm hmm," Quackers said. "And how's your leg?"

"Oh," she said, glancing down, "Nothing."

Quackers gave her a sidelong glance. "What'd you say?"

"My leg is bleeding."

"You're dying."

"No, I'm fine. It's just like when you have to pee and you're dreaming, and you just keep peeing and peeing in your dream and then you wake up and…"

"You peed the bed?" Quackers suggested.

The little girl nodded, a little bit disgusted at the memory. She hadn't peed the bed in years.

"If your leg's already like that here, what do you think it's going to be like when you wake up?"

"I don't know," the little girl said. "I don't want to wake up. I just want to stay here."

Quackers stepped off her chest and cuddled under her armpit. "I'd really like it if you stayed here with me, but you can't."

"Why not?" she asked. "I don't want to go back."

"You can't stay here. You have to go back and stop the Thing Under Your Bed from getting loose. You have to do whatever it takes to keep it trapped."

The little girl was about to ask what she could possibly do, but before her very eyes Quackers's feathers turned from bright yellow to an ashen gray. She turned to look beyond the wood line, past where all of the ducklings were settled in piles, snoring. Something lurked there in the dark bowers of the forest, something without eyes or a face, or hands, or tentacles, but somehow all of them and more.

Fighting against the overwhelming pressure of the sleep paralysis on her chest, the little girl snatched Quackers into her arms, but a far stronger force was yanking the bird out of her arms.

THE THING UNDER YOUR BED

"It's here!" she cried out. "It's here, too! We have to get out of here, Quackers. We have to fly far, far away."

Quackers shook her head from side to side mournfully. She spoke, but not in her voice. It was Dad's voice. "There'll be no more flying for us, cuddlebug."

"Why not?" she moaned, cursing how childish her voice sounded.

But no answer came. No answer in comprehensible words, in any case. Quackers was shrieking in pain. Her shrieks rose in pitch and alarm, and the little girl quivered, trying to pull her friend to safety, but realizing with a sickening moan she was doing the exact opposite.

The bones in Quackers's wings began to separate, crack, and part. Feathers flew in a bloody mockery of a pillow fight, and a sickening series of squishes and crunches resounded through the night air. Quackers came apart in the little girl's arms, but her shattered and useless wings were just the beginning.

"No!" the little girl cried out, tears streaming down her face.

All around her, the little mounds of ducklings began to stir into wakefulness.

Good. At least they'd be able to get away. The Thing couldn't devour them all. She might lose Quackers, but her flock of children would be all right.

"Mommy?" one of the little ducklings asked with a yawn.

The duckling exploded into its component parts in a crimson puff. The Thing wasn't limited here. Perhaps it wasn't limited in the real world, either. She had seen it devour Dad and Freckle both with disarming ease.

Here, though, she watched in mounting horror, as the ducklings began pouring out of their little sleeping piles, all darting in a million directions at once. Then, as if in slow motion, the Thing's non-existence reached out and consumed them each, one by one, with a wet squelch.

Somehow the Thing left Quackers for last. Lame, ruined, her wings destroyed, weeping in the little girl's arms, the mother of all those little ducklings had to watch as her entire family was consumed in front of her. And the little girl could do nothing to stop any of it.

With a final, forceful yank, the duck was wrenched out of the little girl's arms. Screaming bloody murder, and leaving a crimson trail of blood behind her as she was ripped away, Quackers disappeared into the absolute darkness of the tree line.

Fighting to overcome the pressure even now pinning her down, the little girl struggled to her feet. She scanned the darkness, hoping for a sign that Quackers was all right. She strained her ears listening for any sound from her friend.

Terrified, she felt her heart jackhammering in her chest. Not knowing what else to do, she took a few steps toward the wood line.

"Quackers?" she whispered.

A brief, strangled quack called her attention skyward. The duck was floating, suspended in the air a few feet above the little girl's head. The shattered stubs of her missing wings flapped in a mockery of movement, but she could no longer fly. She was held in place by some appendage of the Thing, and the little girl could tell by the way Quackers's bill was attempting to flutter, that her mouth was being held closed, too. She couldn't speak, couldn't squawk, couldn't relate any final words of wisdom. She just floated there in mid-air like some obscene marionette, terror in her tiny, animal eyes.

"Don't panic," the little girl whispered, "I'll get you out of here. I just have to find a ladder or something."

She turned around, scanning the campsite for something to use, but couldn't find anything. When she turned back around, Quackers – what was left of her, anyway – lay in a heap on the ground, her neck twisted fifteen times into knots, her body squished nearly into paste, her legs shattered, bones sticking out and pointing in random directions.

Something wrapped around the little girl's ankle. She tried to cry out, but something else was covering her mouth. Something sticky, slimy, and quivering like syrup. She fell backwards as the Thing yanked her into the wood line. As she fell, her head bashed against the rock of the firepit and she blacked out.

Pain.

The little girl knew pain before she knew anything else.

Dull.

Throbbing.

The next thing she felt, strangely enough, was her mouth. It was bone dry. She tried to speak, but her tongue felt like sandpaper rubbing against cotton.

She tried to swallow, almost thought she would choke, then tried to stop swallowing, and realized how hard it was to stop midway through, as well. She threw herself down on her pillow, tears streaming readily down her face, and slowly worked through the torture of what felt like forcing a lump of charcoal down her gullet, then resolved not to swallow again for as long as she could.

She felt hot. Way too hot for the cool summer night that surrounded her. She reached up to wipe the sweat away from her forehead, but was surprised to find her head was ice cold. Worse than that, glancing down, she saw her arm was whiter than the still-clean portions of her sheets. She tried to move and a thunderbolt of agony snapped through her.

Her pajama pants were missing. With a quivering hand she poked at her thigh and hissed. The thigh was wrapped up, tight, a little bit too tight, really, with what had previously been her pajama pants, torn into small bandages.

The movement made her wince, and she grabbed at her elbow. Though it stung to the touch, it wasn't too bad. The main thing was her thigh.

A pile of Bundrick sat at the foot of her bed. He glanced up darkly at her pained noises.

"You did this?" she wheezed, her voice dusky and weak.

"Did what?" the Thing asked.

"Fuck you," she spat at it, an electric thrill running through her as she used the absolutely verboten language that she had never dared to utter before, not even when she was totally alone.

"Aww, don't be that way," the Thing grunted at her. "I know things have passed between us. But let's call a truce, okay?"

"No!" she snapped. "You…you…"

She didn't want to say it. It sounded too stupid to be worrying about something that had happened in a dream. Easy enough to focus on all the wrongs the Thing had genuinely committed: Freckle, Dad, shooting her.

"I killed your duck friend?" The little girl was silent. The Thing chuckled. "What, you didn't think I knew about that? You weren't dreaming about me. I was in your dream. Consuming the little bits and pieces of your brain that make you happy. Oh, yes, that was a delicious little duck. Too bad you'll never dream about her again. But my belly is full, at least."

The little girl felt an edge of panic tugging at her chest. She tried to ignore it, forcing herself to breathe.

"I…" she stammered, "I can't…"

"Are you thirsty?" the Thing asked suddenly.

"No," she tried to say, but it came out more like a choked wheeze.

"Here," the Thing said, "have a drink."

A small glass seemed to levitate up from the carpet. She watched it carefully, focusing more on what was happening around it than the glass itself, although she had never seen the glass before.

She tried to focus on what she assumed was a tentacle gripping, or possibly simply lifting the glass upward. But she couldn't see anything. It wasn't invisible, like seeing through a window. No, it was like her vision seemed to spread out around whatever she was looking at and avoid it altogether. The Thing existed, but it couldn't be seen.

And so she watched on, in silent shock, as the glass of water slowly levitated up to the side of her bed.

"Go ahead," the Thing said, "take it."

She sat there, reeling in her pain and desperately thirsty, but not wanting to give the Thing the satisfaction. After a moment it chuckled.

"Well, you can't blame a guy for trying. Still, I do want to call a truce. Here, take this."

The Thing set the glass on the edge of her mattress. The little girl eyeballed it for a moment. She couldn't see the hand or tentacle or whatever it was that surrounded the glass, but the Thing was clearly there in some capacity. Why could it reach so far, but no

THE THING UNDER YOUR BED

further? Why was her mattress absolutely sacrosanct, and yet it could shoot up through it at her, and dangle a glass even on the side of her bed?

The Thing grunted a few times in exertion and pushed the glass more than halfway onto her bed. Only then, when she knew she could put her fingers on the glass without breaking the invisible plane, did she dare to snatch up the glass of water. She examined it carefully. It wasn't one of Mom's. She had never seen anything like it before. She stared into the bottom of the glass.

There was something down there, deep below. She lifted the glass up over her head, wincing at her elbow. Looking at the glass from the bottom she could see a mark. It was a little bit like a hippo, but mostly it was just a little curved design. No, she had never seen it in Mom's pantry, but she had seen it before, at her friend's houses, once at the beach. It was a perfectly ordinary, terrestrial glass after all.

"Wait," Bundrick said.

She looked down at him. He was tugging on her night shirt, practically wringing it like a wet rag.

"What?" she tried to hiss.

"It might be poisoned," Bundrick said, but the thought sounded ridiculous, even to her.

"Poisoned?"

"Oh, pfft," the Thing muttered, blowing a raspberry. "I wouldn't poison you. What good would that do me? You know I need to devour you, soul and all. Poisoning would just leave you…well, dead."

She looked to Bundrick, hoping for her trusted guardian/plaything to grant her some insight into the situation. Instead, the rabbit simply shrugged, apparently as exhausted here at three dot dot two two in the morning as she was.

"I'm too thirsty not to," she said flatly, knowing they would probably be the last words she would say, whether she drank the water or not.

Bundrick hung his head in quiet acquiescence.

She greedily gulped down half the glass before forcing herself to stop. She nodded at Bundrick as if to say, "the water's okay." Reluctantly, she put the glass down on top of her light brown headboard. She could have downed every drop just then, but something tickling the back of her brain told her to save what was left or she'd regret it.

"You doing better?" the Thing asked solicitously.

"Where did you get that glass?" she whispered, her voice not quite juicy again, but stronger than it had been.

Bundrick shook his head, indicating that she shouldn't interact with the Thing. But it was too late.

"Oh," the Thing said, "I guess I forget."

She didn't want to be drawn into this discussion, but somehow she allowed herself to be. "You forget?"

"Well, sure," the Thing said. "I've had to terrorize thousands of you people."

"Thousands?" she asked.

"Easily."

Huffing in pain, she threw herself on her belly and crawled down to the other end of the bed so she could avoid moving on her hurt leg. She snapped up Bundrick and pulled the bunny into her embrace, kissing him on the top of his head.

"Thanks for fixing me up," she whispered.

Bundrick stared up at her. "What makes you think I did it?" the bunny asked.

"My pleasure," the Thing said, taking credit for the water, she assumed. "Of course…" it continued, then suddenly trailed off.

"Of course what?" she asked after a moment, deciding she needed more time to recover as the world swirled around her painfully.

"Well," the Thing admitted as if revealing a great secret, "I do like to pop up here and there every night. But it's only once every year that I have to feed. I mean, truly feed, on a family and their concerns. Otherwise it becomes a little bit too obvious to your authority figures."

"And that's me. And my family." She stated it more than asking a question.

"Yes," the Thing admitted, dragging the syllable out far longer than necessary.

Bundrick began struggling in her embrace. She held the bunny tighter. Partially, she didn't want to hear his protests. But also she just needed to squeeze her stuffed rabbit right now.

"Lucky me," she said.

"Hmm, yes," the Thing said, "Of course, you're making this take a lot longer than it's supposed to. What is your hope here? To outlast me? To outwit me?"

"I don't know," she admitted, petting Bundrick's ears down, "What happens if I make it to morning?"

"Then I come back tomorrow," the Thing Under Her Bed growled, "And if you make it the next night, I come back the night after that, and again and again, until your everything is destroyed. And if you leave, I follow you. And if you lock yourself up, I follow you there, too. You can't beat me."

"Maybe I can," Bundrick said.

She glanced down. Reluctantly, she released her grip on the stuffed rabbit. Bundrick turned and pointed with his fingerless hand toward the doorway.

"If you can toss me through the doorway," Bundrick explained, "I know where your father keeps the gasoline and matches. You and your mother won't survive. But that Thing won't be able to escape, either. It'll burn up. Then it won't be able to harm anyone else ever again."

She had burned herself once by touching the coil on the stove. The coil had been glowing red, but she had just been a toddler and hadn't known what that meant.

Her fingertip had blistered instantly. She hadn't even felt any pain in that first instant, had seen the blister, in fact, before feeling anything. So, she'd tried to yank her hand away, but it wouldn't come loose. She had sizzled it stuck to the coil.

With a second yank, it had come free, and left behind a little patch of her finger, blackening on the coil. Then the pain had struck. It had plagued her for weeks and weeks. Dad had told her to soak her finger in milk. Every time she did her finger had felt better, but only for a few seconds.

THE THING UNDER YOUR BED

The whole experience was viscerally real to her, even now, years later. Her fingertip was still a little deranged and she could remember the pain so clearly it was like she could reach out and touch that stovetop any time in her imagination.

A fire would be like that, only over every inch of her body. And who knew how long it would take to die that way? It was a horrifying thought. But, really, was it any scarier than being eaten by that beast down there?

"How's your throwing arm?" Bundrick asked, snapping her out of her reverie.

"I don't know," she admitted, her eyes still locked on her fingertip. It still ached from the glancing shotgun blast.

"Don't know what?" the Thing grumbled angrily, "What am I not making clear here?"

"How's your aim?" Bundrick tried again.

She shrugged. Her heart was fluttering. She felt like a broken-down little puppy, one who had been beaten too hard for too long. Not like Freckle, who had always been happy-go-lucky…but, of course, Freckle was gone now.

"Well, it's up to you," Bundrick said. "We both know what will happen if you miss and I land on the floor inside the room. That Thing will destroy me."

She snatched Captain Bundrick up and crushed him in her grip. For a moment, he seemed just like an ordinary stuffed bunny again.

"I can't lose you," she whispered, smashing his face into her neck.

The Thing growled, lower and angrier than she'd ever heard before. "You are getting on my last nerve."

The bed shook. Tendrils of emptiness seemed to be leaking out from the nether-universe below. The bed shook again. The Thing must have been making a titanic effort. Why couldn't it move the bed? If it was strong enough to tear Dad and Freckle and even her dreams to shreds, why couldn't it just enter her world?

She looked to Bundrick. The bunny was still limp in her arms, but he gave her a determined look.

"There's no good decision," Bundrick admitted, "but there is one correct decision."

She nodded, finalizing her absolute commitment to Bundrick's plan in her mind.

Then the left side of the bed rose almost five inches.

Her arms flailed and, in doing so, reminding her how recently she'd been shot. She practically went flying off the right edge of the bed and for a single, nauseating second she was poised to pitch to the carpet. The tawny Berber carpet yawned before her like a bottomless chasm.

The Thing was audibly straining with all its might. Forcibly regaining her balance, she threw her shoulders against the headboard. She tried to steady herself without grabbing the edges of the headboard, because that would have put her fingers hanging off the edge of the bed.

The Thing grunted and the bed fell back to earth with a loud thunk.

THE THING UNDER YOUR BED

"Get down here!" it roared. "I can smell those lungs, that hair, those tonsils. Every bit of you is going to squiggle down my throat, slippery and wet, like a clam."

The right side of the bed lifted, and this time the Thing had momentum on its side. The bed rocked back and forth. She wasn't going to be able to hold on long.

"Will you at least be able to get away?" she asked Bundrick. "I don't think I could stand losing everyone I care about."

"I can't make any promises, but I'll try," he said.

She got to her knees and held Bundrick over her shoulder, preparing to toss him. Her arms were shouting in agony. The bed was still rocking and she suddenly lost her balance. Screeching, she grabbed two handfuls of mattress to brace herself. Bundrick dropped to the mattress. She saw with burgeoning alarm that just the tiniest tip of his ear was hanging over the corner of the bed.

"Ah ha!" the Thing snapped.

She practically dove to save her only friend left in the world. The Thing stopping to gloat had given her the split second she needed. Bundrick's ear yanked away hard, a puff of cotton going up in the air, but she had just barely managed to grab the rest of him.

"Bundrick!" she shouted.

"I'm all right," he said with a wet cough. "First I gave my eye for the cause, and now an ear."

"I've had a little taste of hasenpfeffer now," the Thing growled, "and it was de-e-e-licious. I'll tell you what: one final offer. Toss the rabbit down and I'll let you and your mother live."

Bundrick had the petrified look of a real rabbit pinned by a predator.

"What?" she whispered.

"Rabbit for your life," the Thing said. "Cross my heart and hope to die. What do you say?"

"Don't listen to it," Bundrick said. "You agreed to only listen to me."

"Well," she said, weighing her options, "why would you want that?"

"Oh, it's not ideal. But that thing is soaked with all of your delicious phobias and juicy delusions. I know you don't entirely understand, but I don't just feed on your body. It's the way your body tastes afraid or, better yet, utterly demented. And that rabbit is your own personal trauma sponge. It would be akin to trading a Thanksgiving feast for a package of those orange vending machine peanut butter crackers, but it's better than nothing."

Looking around she realized Bundrick had snuck out of her embrace and was down at the foot of the bed, cringing away from her. He held up his hands.

"Now, wait! Wait just a minute. We've been friends all your life. Do you remember when you got me?"

She licked her lips and nodded. "Of course."

"Really?" the Thing responded. "You agree?"

She hesitated, enough for Bundrick to take notice.

"Focus," he said. "Remember when we first met?"

THE THING UNDER YOUR BED

She nodded. It was her earliest memory, actually. Mom and dad had taken her to a carnival. Her parents had still been happy then. Mom hadn't begun drinking herself to death. Dad hadn't yet shacked up with whoever "that whore" Mom always complained about was. The tiny family had walked down the street together as one, with one of the little girl's hands in each of her parent's.

Then she had spotted it: a game of tossing tennis balls at what Dad had explained were old-fashioned milk cartons, except metal. Instantly she was obsessed. She had watched as a boy of maybe eighteen had tossed six balls and missed every time.

Captain Bundrick had been hanging from the very highest pin in the stand, though, of course, she hadn't named him that yet. He had just been some bunny. But she had spotted him instantly and recognized him as a present representing the absolute pinnacle of success.

"Yes," Bundrick said out loud, as though following along hand-in-hand with her on her stroll down memory lane.

"What's going on up there?" the Thing asked. "I won't offer you another deal. I'm coming up."

"Oh, shush!" she said. "If you could do that, you would have already."

The Thing hissed and moaned, rocking the bed a few times again, but this time to much weaker effect. She returned to the theater of her mind.

Dad had offered to knock over the milk bottles for her. She had almost let him, too. She had been far too little to throw a tennis ball. But she had insisted that she wanted to play the game. So, admiring her dedication, Dad had ponied up the five bucks or whatever exorbitant amount the carnie running the booth had requested.

Back in the here and now she whispered, "Dad," a tear falling down her cheek, but preferred to return to the time when he had been alive.

Her first throw hadn't even reached the table where the milk bottles sat. Her second ball had been a little better. Then, with the third, she had struck the milk bottles dead on, shocking the carnie into stunned silence. Dad had laughed uproariously and lifted her up onto his shoulders so that she could pluck one of the bunnies – her Captain Bundrick – down herself.

"And I've been with you ever since," the rabbit said when her recollections had faded, "Through every scraped knee, every long, scary night. Haven't I always been there?"

"You were willing to sacrifice yourself before," she said.

"Yes," he agreed, "For the good of the world. To destroy that Thing. But how do you know it won't just come back tomorrow night? Or if not for you, then just move on and torment someone else. Do you want others to have to go through what you're going through now?"

"No," she admitted.

"No?" the Thing repeated in exasperation.

"No, not no, just…give me a minute," she said.

"Take all the time in the world, why don't you?" the Thing grumbled.

THE THING UNDER YOUR BED

She took a deep breath and picked up the now quivering rabbit. He was shaking so hard in her arms it reminded her of the time Freckle had been to the vet for shots and started howling in pain and sought comfort in her arms...

No. She didn't want to think about that, either.

"Shh, shh," she said, running her hand down the whole of Bundrick's back.

In her hands he felt like a real rabbit. She had petted one once, at the pet store. Come to think of it, Captain Bundrick had been with her then. She had declared loudly after Mom wouldn't agree to let her have a real rabbit that she preferred Captain Bundrick anyway.

And she had. They'd been fast friends for almost her whole life now. She couldn't bear the thought of being without him. He'd been with her for her first day of school, in spite of the scorn she had received from the older kids for bringing what they had called a "woobie" with her. They had discovered the bridge in the park beyond the backyard together. The idea of being without Bundrick was simply intolerable to her.

"Come on, little morsel," the Thing growled, "give him to me. Or give yourself to me. Time to make a decision."

She nodded. She already had.

She rose, struggling, all the way to her feet, forming two imprints in the mattress.

"Please don't do this to me," Bundrick said. "You need me. Don't even think of me. Just think of yourself. What will you do without me?"

80

She shut her eyes. It was probably foolish to do so, but she couldn't bear to watch. Grunting, she drew her arm back and tossed the stuffed rabbit with all her might, fighting right through the pain in her elbow as though it weren't even there.

She paused, listening, taking in everything: the steady hum of the cicadas, the occasional lonesome wail of a cat, the barely audible flickering of the television downstairs. The entire symphony of nighttime.

Then, with a deep breath, she opened her eyes.

"No no no!" the Thing moaned. "That's too far! I can't reach it out there. What are you, stupid?"

With a titanic effort she felt the entire foot of the bed rise, inch after inch, almost a foot off the ground. The Thing let it drop with a massive thud. Her teeth chattered in her head and she windmilled her arms, wishing she weren't standing. The entire bed bucked back and forth. The lower left corner lifted, then the upper right.

She dropped to her knees. The Thing was furious. All around her, the moonlight disappeared as the Thing's presence expanded throughout her room. She had felt it before – that absolute absence of anything. Now, something else punctuated the emptiness: malice. The Thing was filled with an unknowable rage, a thwarting of its vision.

It was trying, with all its hate, to break through into her reality.

"I have been lurking in the shadows throughout eternity," it groaned as her bed swayed wildly through the air, and she feared all four legs had lifted off the

THE THING UNDER YOUR BED

ground simultaneously. "When man laid his head on a rock as a pillow, I was lurking in the back of his cave. And I stole little children from the tombs of the Egyptian pharaohs millennia ago. I was the source of every nightmare and fairy story that plagued the Dark Ages. And all for such a tiny price: a small offering, once a year, never too much. Just a child to glut myself on, maybe her family, too, in lean times, and in return I held this door. Do you have any idea what forces wait beyond for you? Any idea of the fecund, gargantuan monstrosities which stalk this plane?"

She didn't know if any other children had ever vexed it the way she had in all the years it claimed to have been doing this, but judging from its reaction, the answer was no.

The side of her bed rose so high she was practically vertical. Below her feet she could see the absence of everything below, yawning, a pit beneath her, and still could see nothing of the monster, not the red eyes Dad had mentioned, not the slithering mass of appendages she had sensed in the air, just the malice, the pure hate.

She clutched at the side of the bedrail. She was nearly hanging off it. Somehow, the Thing still couldn't pass through. She glanced at the bedroom door.

Bundrick was gone.

She nodded. All right. Now it was up to her to keep the Thing busy until Bundrick was done. She had to hold on. Hold on, not for dear life, that was already forfeit, but for the lives of others.

"Come to me!" it wailed. "Come into me!"

With a yank and a heave, she pulled the mattress from its spot and flung it downward. The bed clattered to rest, nearly diagonal from its original position, but more or less on all fours. The screws holding the frame together had been shaken nearly out of their slots. The left bedrail was all at cross angles.

And on the floor, the mattress was messily exploding into ribbons and splinters of metal. A spring flew out, and nearly struck her in the eye, but she ducked, grabbing her pillow and holding it up to shield her face. She crouched on the box spring, which was harder than the mattress, and so made her feel a little safer, but was also much less comfortable.

An unearthly scream filled the air. Great claw marks rent the carpet, exposing the gray material beneath. A punch nearly shoved the box spring up into her. Then another, then another. The material was beginning to give. And the slats beneath, the only thing between her and the dark emptiness welling up below, were splintering and crunching audibly. Soon her weight and the box spring's would be too much for the slats. She'd slip away and disappear into the Thing's realm.

"Mom!" she cried out in desperation.

"Mom! Mom! Motherfucking cocksucking bitch Mom!" the Thing roared in crazed mockery and anger.

Crunch.

Crunch.

Crunch.

Before today she'd never counted how many wooden slats lay across the bedrails. Now she knew

THE THING UNDER YOUR BED

there were exactly six. There were six loud snapping crunches, after maybe twice as many hard jabs from the Thing below.

Now nothing held the box spring in place except the bedrails. She could already feel the entire rectangle of fabric sagging under her weight. This was it. There was nothing else to do. Not even the tiniest scrap of hope between her and utter doom.

She pinched her eyes shut.

"You should have taken me up on one of my offers. Your mother could have lived. You could have, too, you little shit. Now you're going to suffer like no one ever has."

The unmistakable scent of gasoline filled the air. Like a shot, her eyes snapped open. In the doorway stood Bundrick, a triumphant figure, silhouetted in light, and carrying what was unmistakably a jerry can. He stood in an ever-widening puddle of fuel.

"Bundrick!" she cried out in glee.

"What?" the Thing roared, distracted from its final dark meditations.

Bundrick struck a match. The little girl sighed in contentment as a wall of flames licked over her room, blackening the flesh from her bones.

The next day, the fire department reported an entirely different explanation for the blaze.

THE END

NOTE FROM THE PUBLISHER

Thank you for reading *The Thing Under Your Bed.* Whether you liked it or not, we hope you'll take a moment to leave a review on Amazon or your favorite book review site. Reviews are vitally important, both to help us market the book and to help the author improve their writing. Thank you!

ACKNOWLEDGEMENTS

Gavin Dillinger and Kenny Hughes did some of the tremendous work of pre-reading this work.

While researching whether this book was in any way original, I came across Brandon Shane's webcomic "The Monster Under the Bed." He was very encouraging to me in this endeavor.

My thanks go out to Sharon Wasko, a truly extraordinary cover artist, and to Kayleigh Marie Edwards, my secret atomic superweapon.

All my gratitude for everything positive in my life goes out to my partner, Amy Lower.

ABOUT THE AUTHOR

Stephen Kozeniewski (pronounced "causin' ooze key") is a two-time winner of the World Horror Grossout Contest. His published works have been nominated for several Splatterpunk, Voice Arts, and Indie Horror Book Awards, among other honors. He lives in Pennsylvania with his girlfriend and their two cats above a fanciful balloon studio.

Look for These Exciting Books from French Press!

☐ *Billy and the Cloneasaurus* _____ $2.99
☐ *The Ghoul Archipelago* _____ $2.99
☐ *Braineater Jones* _____ $2.99
☐ *Broken-Down Heroes* _____ $2.99
☐ *You're Mine* _____ $2.99
☐ *Illusions of Isolation* _____ $2.99

Please send me the French Press books I have checked above. Enclosed please find my PayPal of $_____ to the French Press account.

Name: _____
E-mail Address: _____
eBook Format: ☐ .pdf   ☐ .epub   ☐ .mobi

Back in the '80s and '90s this was literally how you ordered books. You ripped out the last page in the back of the book you were reading and then mailed it to the publisher. I know, right?

Well, guess what? I'm bringing it back. I mean, not literally. I'm not giving out my home address or anything. But, what the hell. If you want to e-mail me, I'll send you the e-books you want and cut out the middleman. It'll be sort of like a hefty dose of nostalgia, but for the modern age. Screencap this page or whatever and send it to:

frenchpresspub@hotmail.com

Six billion identical clones make up the entire population of Earth, and William 790-6 (57th Iteration) is exactly like everybody else. In his one year of life he will toil in suburban mediocrity and spend as much cash as possible in order to please his corporate masters. When 790's first birthday (and scheduled execution) finally rolls around, a freak accident spares his life.

Living past his expiration date changes 790 profoundly. Unlike other clones he becomes capable of questioning the futility of his own existence. Seeking answers in the wilderness, he discovers a windmill with some very strange occupants, including a freakish, dinosaur-like monstrosity. Which is especially strange since every animal on earth is supposed to be extinct…

Dark, haunting, and blisteringly satirical, *Billy and the Cloneasaurus* is the story of one "man's" attempt to finally become an individual in a world of copies.

After ravenous corpses topple society and consume most of the world's population, freighter captain Henk Martigan is shocked to receive a distress call. Eighty survivors beg him to whisk them away to the relative safety of the South Pacific.

Martigan wants to help, but to rescue anyone he must first pass through the nightmare backwater of the Curien island chain.

A power struggle is brewing in the Curiens. On one side, the billionaire inventor of the mind-control collar seeks to squeeze all the profit he can out of the apocalypse. Opposing him is the charismatic leader of a ghoul-worshipping cargo cult. When a lunatic warlord berths an aircraft carrier off the coast and stakes his own claim on the islands, the stage is set for a bloody showdown.

To save the remnants of humanity (and himself), Captain Martigan must defeat all three of his ruthless new foes and brave the gruesome horrors of...*The Ghoul Archipelago*.

The undead private eye everybody calls "Braineater Jones" has an axe to grind. Somebody plugged him and dumped his corpse in a swimming pool.

Worse yet, his memory's gone. He has no idea who killed him or why.

But he's damn sure going to find out.

With a smartass severed head as a partner, Jones hangs up his shingle in the city's undead quarter. When he's not solving cases (poorly) Jones is always looking to keep his flask full.

Prohibition is in full swing, and the dead need alcohol to function. Without liquor they become mindless, flesh-munching ghouls. (In a word: braineaters.)

Everything will probably be fine. The investigation into his own murder probably won't point Jones toward the city's most important bootlegger.

And even if it does, it's not like he'll risk cutting off the hooch just to seek justice for himself, right? No one man's life is worth unleashing a cannibalistic orgy of violence. Right?

Cracking this case will be a tall order, but one thing's for sure: whatever happens, Braineater Jones isn't getting out of this one alive…

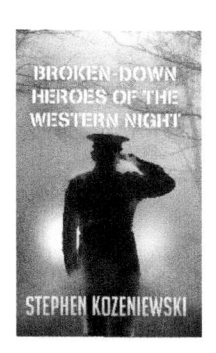

Hardcharging army lieutenant Bickham Deth's only desire is to lead soldiers in combat. In the bloody winter of 2006, he expects to finally earn his baptism by fire on the streets of Kabul or Baghdad.

Instead, he finds himself trapped in Oklahoma on funeral detail.

Deth is honored to pay tribute to the veterans of Vietnam and World War II, but his patience is pushed to the breaking point by incompetent morticians, squabbling family members, and a mishap with the color of his socks that threatens to derail his entire military career.

As the "needs of the army" turn a three-day task into a never-ending odyssey, Deth finds solace from his grim work in the gallows humor of his partner, Sergeant Bela Packs. In his fifteen years of service Packs has seen it all, and his war stories are a welcome distraction from the painful task of burying the dead.

As the honors team weaves its way through the American heartland, seeing both the sublime and ugly sides of small town life, Packs unravels the spellbinding tale of the worst Soldier who ever lived...

Insecure misfit Ioni Davis never thinks she'll find love in her sleepy West Virginia hometown. Then the tall, fascinating stranger Raber Belliveau transfers to her school.

Their attraction is instant and red-hot. And a shared fascination with witchcraft bonds the young lovers even closer.

But while Ioni is responsibly studying her newfound religion of Wicca, Raber has chosen an altogether…different path.

Soon, Raber's behavior becomes manipulative. Even abusive. And their love story for the ages is turning into a macabre farce. All Ioni wants to do is get out.

But Raber has discovered a dreadful way to control their relationship. A ritual which hasn't been attempted in over a century. A spell to unleash a bloodthirsty terror which can never be satisfied.

Ioni finds herself trapped in a struggle for her life and even her free will against a once-trusted lover who has assured her…

You're Mine.

Is anyone ever really alone?

When a young man's wife goes away for the weekend, he lies awake all night wondering what the otherworldly sound in the attic is and why only he can hear it.

After her husband's death, a mother who interacts with her son exclusively through stationery notes grapples with the strange ways her lost love seems to be haunting them both.

And inch by inch, room by room, a young girl's home is overtaken by a savage jungle, even while her parents are being gradually replaced by somewhat…wilder housemates.

In this debut collection Brennan LaFaro, the author of *Noose* and *Slattery Falls*, brings you these stories of creeping dread and much, much more. Contained within are thirteen tales of horror, humor, and heart, (including nine which have never before seen the light of day) and an introduction by the legendary Jonathan Janz.

Is anyone ever really alone? Or are they merely suffering…

Illusions of Isolation?

Printed in Great Britain
by Amazon